SO-DUW-233

STEPHANIE SIMPSON MCLELLAN

SULLY
Messed Up

Red Deer Press

SULLY
Messed Up

Published in Canada by Red Deer Press,
195 Allstate Parkway, Markham, ON   L3R 4T8

Published in the United States by Red Deer Press,
311 Washington Street, Brighton, MA 02135

Red Deer Press acknowledges with thanks the Canada Council for the Arts
and the Ontario Arts Council for their support of our publishing program.
We acknowledge the financial support of the Government of Canada
through the Canada Book Fund (CBF) for our publishing activities.

Edited for the Press by Peter Carver
Text and cover design by Tanya Montini
Proudly printed in Canada by Houghton Boston

Library and Archives Canada Cataloguing in Publication

Title: Sully, messed up / Stephanie Simpson McLellan.
Names: Simpson McLellan, Stephanie, 1959- author.
Identifiers: Canadiana 20200362070 | ISBN 9780889956377 (softcover)
Classification: LCC PS8575.L457 S85 2021 | DDC jC813/.6—dc23

Publisher Cataloging-in-Publication Data (U.S.)

Names: Simpson McLellan, Stephanie, 1959-, author.
Title: Sully, Messed Up / Stephanie Simpson McLellan.
Description: Markham, Ontario : Red Deer Press, 2021. | Summary: "First day of Grade 9 is a
literal horror for Sully. He can't seem to find his own face in the mirror, and soon attracts a trio
of bullies at school. He is the perfect target, lacking confidence and with only two other misfits
for friends. It's only when he begins to overcome his fears and see that the friends have much
to offer that he finally discovers his true face" -- Provided by publisher.
Identifiers: ISBN 978-0-88995-637-7 (paperback)
Subjects: LCSH: Bullying-- Juvenile fiction. | Individual differences in adolescence -- Juvenile
fiction. | Friendship in adolescence -- Juvenile fiction. | BISAC: JUVENILE FICTION / Social
Themes / Self-Esteem & Self-Reliance.
Classification: LCC PZ7.M435Sul | DDC [F] – dc23

www.reddeerpress.com

For Trysten,
who is both Sully and Morsixx,
and for Sarah and Eryn,
who fueled the heart and soul of Blossom

CHAPTER 1

"Out of bed this minute, Sullivan Brewster."

Sully woke to the whack of his mother's fist on his bedroom door.

"You're going to miss the bus if you don't get a move on."

He pushed his curtains aside with his foot. Darkness still crouched at the window and clung to the corners of his room.

"Did you hear me?"

"I heard you, Mom. I'm getting up."

"Come on, Sleepybones. You've had all summer to sleep in. You don't want to be late on your first day of Grade 9."

Sully rolled his eyes and rolled over.

"I'm up. I'm up."

"Breakfast in ten. Pedal to the metal, Sullivan."

Untwisting himself from his sheets, Sully stumbled to his feet and hitched up his boxers. He shuffled across the hall and flicked on the bathroom light.

And screamed.

"Sullivan?"

"It's okay, Mom."

It wasn't okay.

Sully jerked back at the sight of something inhuman staring at him from inside the bathroom mirror. The creature in the mirror jolted back at the exact same moment.

Sully thrust his arms in front of his face to push the apparition away. The creature mimicked the gesture in perfect unison. Its muddy brown hair rippled in loose curls to its shoulders in exactly the way Sully's did, and its pasty white skin became whiter still as Sully felt the color drain from his own pale face.

It was wearing Sully's boxers.

Through the weave of his fingers, Sully spied the creature spying at him through the weave of its fingers. With a shriek, he realized he was looking at himself.

But not himself.

Sully leaned into the mirror, meeting his reflection halfway.

His nose, pink and dripping, hunkered sideways on his left temple. One of his ears—it was hard to tell which one from the unfamiliar angle—bulged where his nose should have been. The other protruded, antenna-like, right above his lips, which quivered, post-scream, in the middle of his forehead.

Thinking he might still be asleep, Sully pinched the soft skin on the inside of his arm.

"Ow!"

He rubbed his eyes, one on either side of his chin, and squinted at his reflection again.

Nothing changed. He still looked like a frightened Picasso or deranged Mr. Potato Head. As he watched, the black hole in the middle of his forehead opened wider, spilling shrill sound into his ears, perched just north and south of the eruption.

Sully slapped one hand across his forehead to stop the sound, the other over his chin to block the image. He staggered backward out of the bathroom and tripped across the hallway into his room. Twisted configurations of socks and T-shirts grabbed his ankles, causing him to slide head-first across his bedroom floor on a direct collision course with his dresser.

CHAPTER 2

As he regained consciousness, Sully's left temple twitched at the smell of frying bacon. His *Star Wars* action figures came into focus, knocked to the floor when his head hit the dresser. Luke Skywalker's legs protruded from the waistband of last week's underwear. Darth Vader dug into Sully's right cheek.

The nightmare still fresh, Sully let his fingers crawl up the sides of his face, intrepid explorers torn between hope and fear. They didn't have to go further than his chin to discover the unmistakeable contour of his eyes, before he threw himself sideways. And threw up.

"Breakfast is on the table, Sullivan."

Mom's words, shouted from the bottom of the stairs, might as well have been in a foreign language. They sat in Sully's brain for several seconds before he could decipher their meaning. Mopping dribbles of puke from his forehead, his reply was a barely audible grunt.

He pushed himself to his knees to see his reflection in the dresser mirror.

"Sullivan?" Mom said.

This in reaction to a choked scream Sully muffled by savagely grabbing his forehead as he stared at his reflection.

"I'm not feeling well, Mom. I don't want breakfast."

The scene staring back at him was reminiscent of that painting of the screaming man on the bridge. Sponge Bob stared at him from a poster on the left of his mirror, fractured steel reflections of Billy Talent to the right.

"Open the door, Sullivan." Mom's voice was now mere feet away. "I know you're nervous, but it'll all be fine. I promise."

"I'm not dressed!" Sully threw himself at his bedroom door. He needed time to think before sharing his predicament.

"Seriously, Sullivan. You need to speed it up. Dressed and at the table in two minutes."

"Wake up, Sully. Wake up." Sully slapped his cheeks with both hands, narrowly missing his nose.

He pulled some jeans over his boxers and rummaged through the pile of clothes furthest from the vomit. He found a T-shirt under some underwear and jammed a wool cap over his head. Rearranging his hair so it covered most of his face, he navigated the stairs and skulked into the kitchen.

"So, you had a good sleep?" Mom's back was to him as she scooped eggs onto a plate at the stove.

Sully slid into his seat as inconspicuously as circumstances allowed and contemplated his own breakfast. His stomach felt as messed up as his face, as he tried to logic how to get food into his mouth. Which was on his forehead. Under his cap.

Outwitted by the riddle, he pushed scrambled eggs and bacon around his plate.

"I just want a little."

"Take your hat off at the table, Sullivan." Mom put another plate on the table and turned back to the stove.

"Rooster, look." His little sister, Eva, pushed some bacon into her mouth through her missing front teeth.

Mom handed her a napkin. "Manners, young lady."

"Cool look, Rooster." Eva placed the napkin on her head and pushed her hair in front of her own face. "Twins!" she giggled and swiped at Sully's hat.

"Let your brother eat, Eva," said Mom. "He's got a bus to catch."

Sully slouched sideways and scooped a small forkful of eggs under his hair when no one was looking.

"Your mother said take your hat off, Van, my man." His stepdad, Bill, tousled the top of Sully's head before swinging into the chair across the table.

No sooner had Sully yanked his cap back in place than Eva snatched it herself and jammed it on her own head. "I'm Rooster! I'm Rooster!"

Sully's flying hands were inadequate to cover up his seriously messed up face. His nose sprinted back and forth across his temple. His right eye twitched at the edge of his chin.

"Sullivan!" said Mom.

"Rooster!" said Eva.

"Why, Vanny," said Bill.

Sully curled forward and shut his eyes. He jammed one finger into the ear in the middle of his face and the other in the one on top of his head.

"Seriously, Sullivan." Mom pulled his hands away from his face. "Stop horsing around and eat your breakfast."

"There's something on your face," said Eva.

"Give your brother his hat," said Bill.

"But he's got ketchup on the end of his nose," said Eva.

Sully's hand darted to his left temple to inspect his nose. His stepsister was right. There was a slime of ketchup there. But was that the point?

"Can't you see something's wrong with me?"

"Don't yell at your mother, Vanny," said Bill.

"I'm not kidding," Sully said. "Look at me. Look at my face."

"Don't worry, Rooster," said Eva. "It's just ketchup."

"I'm not talking about ketchup!" Sully's voice tripped across three different octaves in five words.

"Scrambled eggs, too." Eva slid her fingers along some strands of her hair to indicate where Sully should check his own.

"Give your brother back his hat, Princess," said Bill.

"Please," said Mom. "Everyone settle down so we can have a nice family breakfast."

"Can I eat in my room? I really don't feel like myself right now."

"Stay where you are, Vanny." Bill said. "Like your mother said, we're all going to sit together and have a nice breakfast."

"Seriously, Mom. I think I might have leprosy or something."

"Oh, for heaven's sake, Sullivan."

"Don't I look any different to you?"

"Only with your hat on," Eva offered. She nodded at Sully encouragingly.

"Mom, please!" Sully said.

"It's hard to see with your hat and all that long hair." His mom cupped his chin and turned his face to the right and then left, as if sizing up a garage sale find.

"Something really strange is happening." Sully pulled away from his mom. "Look at my face."

"You've just got first-day jitters," she said. "You look perfectly normal to me."

"Except for your hat," tried Eva again. "And the ketchup."

"Eat your breakfast, Eva," said Mom. "Sullivan, there's nothing wrong with you that a good haircut wouldn't cure. Now, everybody stop the dramatics and let's finish breakfast in peace."

Sully slumped back in his chair and slid a piece of bacon into his forehead.

"Doesn't it look strange to you the way I'm eating?" he tried one more time. "Look at my eyes. And my ears. That's definitely not normal!"

"Maybe you got ketchup in your eyes, too?" With a look of concern, Eva leaned forward to peer into Sully's face.

"Look at me, Mom." Sully pawed the sides of his chin. "Look at my eyes. Just look at them. They're not—"

"It might be ketchup," insisted Eva.

"It's not ketchup!" Sully pushed away from the table. "Look, just forget it. I'm fine. Everything's fine. I have to get ready or I'll miss the bus."

"Wait, Rooster." Eva grabbed his arm and jabbed the napkin toward the ketchup on his face.

Sully pulled himself free and bolted up the stairs. After tossing his vomit-soiled clothes in the laundry, he shut his bedroom door and approached his dresser mirror again.

"Can't anyone see what's happened to me?" he whispered.

CHAPTER 3

As his mother predicted, Sully was lucky to catch the bus.

Before he'd even crossed the road en route to his designated stop two blocks away, the school bus barreled past him. Pulling his cap down, his backpack up, and his hair forward, he broke into a sprint down the middle of the road, pacing the big wheels and wheezing with effort.

Faces pooled at the back of the bus and heads poked out the side windows.

"Run, kid!"

"Faster, Brewster!"

"Niner! Niner!"

While he arrived at the bus stop only seconds after the bus did, the driver greeted him with a sigh.

"Seven twenty-six tomorrow, Curly." The driver pointed to the clock on the dashboard. "Got a schedule to keep."

"Sorry." Sully scanned the crowd of smirking faces through the strands of hair that hung in front of his face.

He couldn't see Morty anywhere. Instead, he found himself looking straight into the eyes of six feet of solid muscle. While he'd never laid eyes on him before, Sully had no doubt this was Tank, celebrated linebacker and legendary overlord of Wild Forest Secondary.

Sully's middle school was one of a dozen that fed the local high school. Over the last two years, Tank's reputation had spread to the feeder schools like a swollen river seeps through the streets after a nasty rain.

Tank dragged a hand across his military cut and impaled Sully with narrowed eyes. The stocky kid to Tank's left squinted his own little pig eyes. He took off and then replaced his backward ball cap, after mimicking Tank's hand-dragging gesture.

"Hey, Ox." A wiry kid with matching ball cap, and pants slung halfway down his backside, reached behind Tank to punch Pig Eyes on the shoulder. "It's a real live hippie."

"Shut it, Dodger." Tank raised his hand to accentuate the command.

Sully flinched and jolted backward. Unbalanced,

he staggered to right himself but tripped forward and landed face first in Tank's lap.

A combustion of laughter from behind extinguished even before Sully found himself briefly airborne, landing this time on the bus floor at Tank's feet.

"Find a seat, kid." The bus driver watched through the rear-view mirror as Sully pushed himself to his knees.

"Look at his face." Dodger's exaggerated guffaw revealed irregularly spaced teeth a touch too small.

Sully's hands raced for his face to feel the map of his new reality.

"Is that ketchup on your face?" said Dodger.

"Scrambled eggs for breakfast?" said Ox, pointing at Sully's hair.

If they noticed how rearranged his face was, they weren't saying.

"What's your name?" Tank's expression remained decidedly unamused as Sully pulled himself to standing.

"Who, me?"

"No, the little fairy in front of me."

"Uh ... Sully."

"Sally?"

"No ... Sully. Sullivan."

"You look more like a Sally to me," said Tank.

Ox and Dodger punched each other.

Tank shot a look at their hyena laughter and then focused on Sully again.

"You remind me of someone," said Tank. "Does Sally remind you of anyone, Dodger?"

"Cousin Itt?" said Dodger. "Only curly. Cousin Itt with a curling iron."

"All you losers look the same," said Tank. "That stupid hair can't hide who you are."

"Well, I—"

"Well, I—" Dodger mimicked.

"No one respects someone who doesn't respect themselves, Sally," said Tank. "Do you deserve your own respect?"

Sully's gaze darted right and left, hoping someone might supply him with the correct answer. A strange woman with a big black purse stood on tiptoes outside the bus window with her mouth hanging open. Even she seemed to be waiting for his reply.

"Exactly what I thought." Tank waved his hand in dismissal.

"I can't drive until you sit." The bus driver stood and waved Sully to an empty seat.

Sully shrank backward and into the space indicated.

"Dude," said the kid beside him. "Talk about off to a bad start."

Through strands of hair, Sully spied a tall, lanky boy with long, dark, poker-straight hair, dressed entirely in black, from his skeleton hoodie to his belted, chained knee-high runners. Sully shifted as close to the edge of his seat as he dared without making any part of himself visible to Tank.

"Look at me, Dude. Man, what happened to you?"

Sully's hands flew up to the still unfamiliar landscape of his face.

"I—"

"More like what didn't happen to you. Didn't you do anything this summer besides babysit your sister?"

Sully cocked his head. The voice sounded a lot like Morty's.

"What are you looking at?" The Emo kid tossed back his head. His lips moved perfectly in sync with the sound of his friend's voice.

As Sully looked around to see where Morty was hiding, a purple house sailed in and out of view from the bus window.

"Earth to Sully." The Emo kid snapped his fingers in front of Sully's face.

"Do I know you?"

"Man, you really are out of it this morning. It's Morsixx, Dude."

"Morsixx? Really?" A girl in the seat across the aisle shrilled her surprise. "Is that some kind of warrior name?" Laughing, she tapped her hand to her lips and made a "woo-woo-woo" sound.

"Shhhh," the girl beside her giggled. "I heard his mama's one crazy—" She spoke the taboo insult in a whisper, but loud enough for Morsixx to hear.

Sully looked at the girls in disgust and then back at the boy. He jutted his chin forward and pushed the hair away from his low-lying eyes to get a better look.

"Morty?" It was beginning to dawn on Sully that Morty's voice really was coming out of the Emo kid's mouth.

"Morsixx," the Emo kid said. "I told you that last night. Weren't you listening?"

"Morsixx? ... Wait a minute. Is that really you, Morty? What, did you grow a foot at your dad's over the summer? Why are you dressed like that?"

Sully and Morty's surnames, Brewster and Bearheart, were usually one after the other in alphabetical class lists, so they often sat next to each other in elementary and middle school. Friends more by default than design, they'd decided at the end of last year to share a locker in Grade 9.

"This is just me, Dude."

"No, it's not you, Morty!" Sully's assertion skipped ungracefully from A-minor through F-sharp. He nodded to the back of the bus and then to the girls across the aisle. "Are you trying to get yourself killed?"

"Their bad, Dude. Racial slurs can't touch me. And the name's Morsixx, now." Morty handed Sully a black handkerchief decorated with skulls. "You got ketchup on your face, Dude. Clean yourself up."

CHAPTER 4

Sully bolted from the bus as soon as it stopped. With a plan to avoid any further collision with Morsixx, Tank, or any other human being, he circumvented the locker and headed straight to class. Grade 9 hadn't even officially started, and this day was already a million times worse than the worst of his imaginings.

Passing the cafeteria, he caught his reflection in the darkened glass and shuddered.

He started down the hall and looked back and forth between his timetable and the numbers over the doorways. He turned right and then left before passing a side hallway that ended in a broom closet. A round boy about his age was slumped in a corner by the open closet doorway. With his head in his hands, his shoulders shook with some tragic sniffling.

Sully took a step toward him and then back. He'd

had a bad morning himself. No one could blame him if he decided to simply walk away and not get involved, especially since the boy didn't even know he was there.

He tiptoed backward and darted glances between the emptying hallway and the boy in the broom closet, before he sighed and walked toward him.

"Are you okay?"

The kid's face was gooey with snot when he looked up at Sully's voice. His tongue protruded slightly from his mouth as he sniffed and wiped his nose with short, pudgy fingers.

"Miss Winters said to turn right." The boy raised his right hand. His puffy, soulful eyes studied Sully out of wide, flat features. "But this isn't a classroom."

"I'll take you to the office, okay?"

"Are you a girl?" The boy's face cracked a smile as he reached for Sully's hair. His own dark brown hair was trimmed in a tidy bowl cut.

"What? No!" said Sully. "I'm kind of in a hurry. Do you want me to take you to the office?"

"You have girl's hair," said the boy.

"Yah, yah, I know. Look, follow me, okay? I'll help you find Miss—"

The rest of Sully's sentence was swallowed by the bell.

"That scared me!" The boy jumped. He grabbed Sully's arm and giggled.

"Bell." Sully pointed at the ceiling and then at himself. "I gotta go."

"You're Belle?" said the boy.

"Yes," said Sully. "My bell. I'm late for class. C'mon. I'll take you to the office."

"Like in *Twilight*?" said the boy. "Belle? Like Bella?"

"What?"

"You have curly hair, Bella," said the boy.

"No," said Sully. "My name isn't—"

"There you are, Winston." An older woman came up behind them, her gray bun pulled sharply at her temples to expose hawk-like features.

"Aren't you supposed to be in class, young lady?" She ran her finger across the top and then down the squares of Sully's timetable. "Get a late slip from the office and hurry along."

"Man," said Sully.

"Excuse me?" said the woman.

"Young man," said Sully, "and I was just—"

"She has curly hair." Winston pointed at Sully as the woman ushered him along. "Bye, Bella!"

Flustered, Sully made a full circle to reorient himself.

Off to his right, Tank leaned against a bank of nearby lockers.

"Better hurry along, Sally." Tank pointed at Sully and twitched his thumb to his index finger as if cocking a gun. "Or is it Bella?"

CHAPTER 5

"Girls' Health class is down the hall in room 251, young lady." The muscular middle-aged man with the receding hairline—Mr. Green, according to Sully's agenda—directed a beefy finger out the door over Sully's left shoulder. "Guys only in this class."

"No, I—"

"You heard the man, Sally."

Tank shoved Sully into the room with a broad shoulder as he sauntered in behind him.

"We're going to try this one more time, are we?" Mr. Green looked past Sully and straight at Tank, as if Sully had already trotted down the hall.

"Third time's the charm," said Tank.

After laughing at Sully, the class now turned their attention to the Tank–Green show.

"I thought the boys might want some pointers from

someone who's used their equipment recently." Tank's comment drew whistles and laughs from the class.

"Cocky words from someone who's flunked this class twice. Take your seat." Green directed Tank to a desk in the barren first row and then turned back to Sully. "I said room 251, Miss. Move along."

"Sir, I—"

"Now, then." Green ignored Sully again. "We're just missing Brewster. Any of you know a Sullivan Brewster?"

Tank ambled to the back row and stood in front of a thin kid whose face reddened under his pointed stare. Grabbing his backpack, he'd barely vacated his seat before Tank replaced him.

Shooting a warning glance at Sully, Red Face darted to the last empty seat in the middle row.

"I'm Sullivan Brewster, sir." Sully held up his small yellow late slip as if it was the missing piece to this puzzle.

Green looked surprised to see Sully still in his classroom. "Speak up, young lady." Uproarious laughter issued from everyone but Tank, who was now leaning back with his hands folded behind his head and his eyes half-closed.

"I'm Sullivan Brewster, sir." Sully's statement surfed the scales again.

"I see." Green looked at Sully as if inclined to argue the point. "Well,' he said, "okay, then. Take your seat, Brewster."

Shaking his head, Green walked to the blackboard and wrote Sex Ed in foot-high letters.

"All right then, Gentlemen. Listen up." He stood with his legs apart and one hand on his hip. With the other, he grabbed the whistle that hung from his neck and gave it two sharp tweets.

"This can go one of two ways." With both hands on his hips now, all he was missing was a cape and a letter on his chest. "I can bore you with lectures you're all going to sleep through, or you can teach the class yourself."

He flung his arm out and pointed directly at Sully, whose heart vaulted into his mouth. Which fell open on his forehead.

"Who, me?" Sully's alarm squeaked into the silence that followed Green's words.

"Yes, you, Brewster." Green paused for effect. "And you, and you, and the whole sorry lot of you."

A hum of murmurs and whispers rose behind Sully.

"Well, that's settled, then," Green pronounced. "Thirty students. Thirty topics. PowerPoint presentation. Minimum twenty minutes. First presentation next Monday."

"That can't be legal!" someone protested.

"Here are your topics, Gentlemen." Green ignored the comment and slid the blackboard over to reveal thirty ghastly words he'd chalked in three rows of ten. Words like Gonorrhea. Chlamydia. Condom. Herpes.

"You'll find a basic presentation outline for each of these topics in the handout." Green deposited a stack of paper on Sully's desk. "Take one and pass the rest on, Brewster. Each of you will be responsible for fleshing out one of these topics to present to the class. No pun intended."

No one laughed.

"After each of your presentations, I'll take over to fill in any gaps or correct any misinformation. If you do a good job, my part will be short, and I'll end class early. Capiche?"

Grumbles and murmurs rumbled around the room.

"All right, then. Topics and presentation dates will be drawn by lottery." Green pulled a box out from under his desk. "Grab a slip on the way out."

These were the last words Sully heard clearly for the remainder of the period. His left ear, the one on his head, had picked up a high-pitched ringing from overhead. His right, pointed as it was directly at the blackboard, deflected the sounds that spilled out of Green's mouth.

"You have a problem with time, Brewster?"

A dribble of drool slid from the corner of Sully's mouth before it curved around his ear and into his left eye.

Green's bark in Sully's middle ear jolted him back to attention. Realizing his classmates were filing out, he stood abruptly, which caused his desk to pitch forward and hammer hard into Green's own middle body part.

As Green choked out some indecipherable words, Sully swung his backpack over his shoulder, smacking Green in the side of the head.

"Sir, I ... I mean, I didn't mean—"

"Slip, Brewster," Green managed, grimacing. "Grab a topic on the way out and just go!"

As he raced for the door, Sully collided with the desk. The topic box fell to the floor where it opened and spilled the last presentation slip on the floor.

"Menstruation," it said. "Monday, October 5."

CHAPTER 6

"Hey."

Sully was pretty sure he'd dialed the right number, but it was hard to tell from that single syllable.

"Morty?"

Two phone conversations with Morty in a week is more than he'd had the entire time they'd been in middle school together, but he needed to talk to someone.

"Hey, Dude."

"Morty, it's Sully."

"Morsixx."

"Just quit this whole Morsixx thing, Morty. You're making a fool of yourself."

"Your opinion, Dude."

"What does that even mean, Morty? Morsixx? Really?"

"It's Latin for Death with a nod to the Gods of Punk and Heavy Metal. And it doesn't matter if you approve or not, Dude. I'm happy with who I am."

"Happy with who you are? Right, Morty. Happy people always go around dressing like corpses and calling themselves dead."

"Death, not dead," said Morsixx. "I'm a process, not an event, Dude. All of us are dying."

"Huh?" said Sully.

"The music speaks to me, that's all," said Morsixx. "Billy Talent and BVB, but that's not even the point."

"Well, what is the point, Morty? You heard the girls on the bus this morning. You really want high school to be a repeat of middle school?"

"Look, Dude. Morty would have worried about those things. He *did* worry about them. Morty hadn't grown worthy of the name Bearheart. Morsixx is working hard to earn it."

"So, you think hiding behind a new name is going to solve all your problems? Like it or not, Morty, you're still you."

"That's what you're not getting, Dude. I'm not hiding. And I do like myself. My dad broke himself on other people's arrows. He forgot himself. Taking a new name at different stages of our journey is part of my heritage. My mother taught me that. Morsixx is who I am now."

"I'm telling you, they're going to bully you worse than ever if you keep this up."

"This is just who I am, Dude. I feel good about myself. Get over it."

"Look, never mind about all that. Tank's posted the Naked Niner Prelude video."

"You know you're just playing into his plan by getting all freaked out about it."

"How can you not get freaked out about it? Have you seen it?"

"I gotta admit, the guy's not stupid. Branding it and everything. He's bound to end up some advertising genius or something."

"What are you even talking about? These are real people he's filmed, not some paid actors."

"I'm just saying. He's a thug, but he's not a dumb thug. Think about it. He was a niner himself when he started this whole thing. Bold, right? I mean, way to pre-empt—"

"Geez, Morty, do you even hear yourself? I repeat. His victims are real people. They—"

"All right, all right. So how bad is it?"

"How bad do you think it is? It's a friggin' nightmare. Shouldn't somebody do something about this? It must be against the law or something."

"Did he sign the post?"

"Sign the post? Of course he didn't sign the post. What kind of moron would put his signature on this kind of thing?"

"Exactly," said Morsixx. "Nobody can do anything about it because they can't trace it back to him."

"Well, they may not be able to trace it, but everyone knows that Tank's behind this."

"Proof, Dude. They have no proof."

"Have you got the page up?" Sully clicked the replay button on his own screen. His fingers hovered along his jawline, ready to block out the horrifying image of Gerald Budinski hanging by his feet from the tree limb. Completely naked. Squirming and squealing, with his arms tied to his sides. Gerald's vain attempts to cover himself up were painful to witness.

An alumnus of the same middle school Sully attended, Gerald was the first Naked Niner. The so-called Aftermath video of his attack (full, unedited footage) had quickly achieved viral distribution in Sully's Grade 7 year.

After Gerald was Billy Smithers, the Naked Niner from last year. Different location but same humiliating pose. In both cases, the footage was shot at night, with the poor Naked Niner illuminated by harsh, unflattering flood lights.

A word crawl across the bottom said: *wimps, losers, posers deserve no respect. beware the black spot. u cant hide. u will be exposed.*

The words twisted in Sully's gut. Tank had used at least three of these words to Sully during the ugly bus encounter.

"You better be careful, Morty," he said.

"Morsixx."

"All right. You'd better be careful ... Morsixx. Do you want to see yourself strung up like that? Exposed like that? You're probably on their list already!"

"I'm not a poser, Dude," said Morsixx. "And I'm not a loser or a wimp, either. They don't scare me."

"Well, you should be scared! Geez, Morty ... *Morsixx* ... you fit the profile perfectly, the way you're hiding in that stupid disguise. You should quit it immediately. As in yesterday. Maybe they'll forget all about it and pick someone else."

"Like I said, I'm not hiding anything, Dude," said Morsixx. "This is just me. Maybe it's you who should be careful. You're awful jumpy."

"Me? Jumpy?"

"You sound like a girl, Dude. Get your voice under control."

"Okay, just forget it. But don't say I didn't warn you."

Sully stared at the screen long after hanging up with Morsixx. Gerald, and even Billy, had been caught unawares, he reasoned. No one sees the first one coming, and if there's only been one, there might not be two.

But this year was three, and three seemed inevitable because, as the saying goes, *things come in threes*. Three was inevitable. That's what Sully figured.

Sully hugged his arms close and started when his computer screen went black. His eyes stared back at him from along his jawline. He took in the out-of-place profile of his nose, which protruded from his left cheek, and the twisted grimace of his mouth, frozen like an open wound across his forehead.

"Morsixx better watch himself," he said to the ear in the middle of his face. And then, more softly, as if afraid to speak the words aloud, "And me, too."

CHAPTER 7

It was the middle of the third week before the notes started showing up on the locker Sully shared with Morsixx. While the bizarre, and apparently invisible, rearrangement of Sully's face hadn't changed, Sully found himself cautiously hopeful that the worst was behind him.

Until now.

Emo Fag, said one of the handwritten signs. *Cut yourself*, said another. *Makeup is for queers*. Worst of all was a crudely drawn heart surrounding the words, *Sally loves Emo*.

Winston was already at the locker as Sully and Morsixx approached. He ran his pudgy index finger slowly over the letters.

Sully gave Morsixx a dark look and put a hand on Winston's shoulder.

"It's okay, Winston." He tore the heart sign off the locker. "We'll take care of it."

"Hi, Bella." Winston unscrewed his face from intense concentration. "That's funny. Also dumb."

"Just some punks." Sully darted a look at Morsixx for help. "Don't worry about it."

"They got it wrong." Winston turned back and pointed at the signs. "How silly."

"You're right," said Morsixx. "They're just brainless, aren't they, Winston. You're much smarter than they are."

"Yes!" said Winston. "I'm smarter! Elmo is not a frog."

"That's right." Sully tried to steer Winston away from the locker. "Wait, what?"

"Ellll-mmmmmo. Frrrrr-oggggg." Winston drew out the pronunciation as he ran his finger over the words again.

"Ah," said Morsixx. "There's no fooling you, is there, Dude."

"There's no fooling Winston," Winston grinned, shaking his head and shrugging his shoulders. "Kermit is the frog, not Elmo."

"The whole thing's just silly, isn't it, Winston," said Morsixx.

"Yes. So silly," said Winston. "And dumb, too."

"You got that right," said Sully. "Well, see ya later, Winston."

"Bye Bella. Bye Mor ... Mor ..."

"Later, Dude."

"Predictable." Morsixx tore down the rest of the notes when Winston was out of earshot. "I'm surprised it took them so long. But hey, you handled that better than I thought you would, Dude."

"I'm not handling anything." Sully's angry, bulging eyes made his chin shake. "I'm not handling anything. I told you this would happen. You have to stop this. Stop dressing like that."

"Chill, Dude," said Morsixx. "I figured it would happen, too, but I can handle it. I'm almost a foot taller than Tank's flunkies, and I could take Tank if I had to."

"I'm not talking about you," Sully said. "Have you given a second thought to what this might be doing to *me*? Drawing attention to yourself is drawing attention to me, too, and I don't want it!"

"Thanks for the support, Dude. Remind me why we're friends again?"

"I don't know ... *Morsixx*. 'Morsixx'—what kind of name is that! I agreed to share a locker with Morty. Morty didn't go around with a *kick me* sign on his back.

You're going to get us killed. Worse, you're going to get one of us strung up, and it's not going to be me!"

"Relax, Dude. I don't like it, either, but I'm not going to let them push me around. I'm tired of punks telling me who I should be. I really don't care what they say or do."

"Well, I *do* care, okay? You're not going to drag me down."

"No offense, Dude, but you're dragging yourself down. You can't pin that on me."

"And another thing. You're forgetting that I'm several inches *shorter* than any of them. I definitely don't have the strength to take them on."

Sully glared at Morsixx's black eyeliner, all black clothing, and chains and skulls. His flaring nostrils made his temple throb.

"It's not about that, Dude. It's inner strength you need. Like the frog said, 'Life's like a movie ... write your own ending.'"

"Well, it's not a movie, is it? It's real life. *My* real life."

"Find your inner Kermit, Dude," Morsixx said, smiling. "Winston could teach you a few tricks."

"Whatever," said Sully. "Lock the locker. I don't want to be late for class."

But if Sully had known what was waiting for him in English class, he would have been glad to be late.

CHAPTER 8

With only two years of data, it was difficult to nail a definite trend, but the stats were that Tank staged the Naked Niner within thirteen days of administering the Black Spot. Both Gerald and Billy had been marked during the sixth week of school.

Sully made a decision on the way to Ms. Wippet's English class. If Morsixx wanted to put himself on Tank's shortlist, that was his problem, but for the next three to four weeks, or as long as it took, Sully planned to avoid both Tank and Morsixx. Morsixx was just going to have to understand that some things, like self-preservation, were more important than friendship.

Tank would be more difficult. Green had posted all the assignments on the board, and Sully's presentation on menstruation loomed like a blind pimple.

While Sully had only one class with Tank, he was

unlucky enough to have the same English class as one of Tank's sidekicks, Dodger. As a result, he'd strategically selected an inconspicuous seat halfway back and off-center. There was an empty desk in front of him, and two forgettably normal kids on either side. Dodger sat in the back row on the other side of the room, far enough away, Sully reasoned, that he likely wasn't even aware that Sully was in his class.

"Lord Alfred Tennyson was one of the foremost poets of the nineteenth century." Ms. Wippet made this announcement like she was an anchor on the evening news. "As we think about the role of art in life, let us consider one of Tennyson's most famous poems, 'The Lady of—'"

"Is this English 101?"

A girl stood in the doorway, her left arm flung dramatically before her, sweeping from Ms. Wippet and the blackboard to Dodger and the shelves of books behind him.

Ms. Wippet peered over her glasses at the interruption.

"It is," Wippet said. "And you are ...?"

"Blossom. My name is Blossom. I just moved here."

"What kind of name is Blossom?" someone cracked from the back of the room.

"It's not a *kind* of name at all." Blossom paid no heed to the laughter and stares. "It's just my name."

While slight of frame, there wasn't anything else about Blossom that was slight or minimal. Her dark curly hair, streaked with shades of red, purple, and aqua, hung in thick waves past her waist. She wore a long, flowing, bright pink skirt, a purple scarf, and a tie-dye messenger bag. But even these things were not the most remarkable traits adorning her. Visible beneath the sheer fabric of her long, silver sleeves, and prominent on her face and neck, were intricate tattoos of flowers, leaves, and vines, painted against the light brown of her skin. She was a bright web of color, like a walking tapestry, casting her open gaze around the classroom as if bestowing God's grace.

Sully immediately despised her.

"So, I'm in the right class?" She removed her scarf and tucked it in her messenger bag.

"So it would seem." Wippet punched some keys on her laptop and scanned her screen. "Have you checked in with the office, Miss—"

"Just Blossom," the girl said. "Yes, they know I'm here, thank you. I'll find a seat, then, Ms. Wippet."

Blossom moved like a river, her skirt and her hair

flowing around her as she swept across the classroom on her way to claim one of the empty seats.

Thinking quickly, Sully hoisted his backpack onto the empty desk in front of him. As she started down his row, he leaned forward and rested his head in his hand.

"Is this seat taken?" she said.

"Yes." Sully flushed a fuchsia that rivaled her skirt.

"By whom?" Blossom's dark eyes darted between Sully and the empty chair. "Are you sure this isn't your backpack?"

"No," said Sully. "It's not mine. There's a seat over there."

He pointed vaguely around him and then slouched sideways and away from her.

Blossom didn't move.

"I don't think you're being truthful." She reached for the backpack.

"No," said Dodger, who came up behind Sully. "Sally's not lying. I wondered where I'd left that."

"No, wait." Sully grabbed for the bag, which Dodger, smiling broadly, had shouldered.

"Are you three quite finished?" said Wippet.

"Seat's all yours, Buttercup." Dodger made a flourish with his hand toward the empty seat.

"Blossom," said Blossom.

"Wait a minute." Sully swept his hair away from his forehead to ensure he was heard.

"Enough interruption," Wippet said. "Blossom, take your seat. Class, turn your eyes back to the board. Now, where were we?"

Blossom swished into the seat in front of Sully. She lifted her hair away from her neck as she settled, so it rippled in waves down her back.

"But—" said Sully.

"Thank you for finding my bag, Sally." Dodger patted the bag protectively. "I'll take good care of it from now on."

"Is your name really Sally?" Blossom turned around and whispered louder than necessary, given that she was mere inches from the ear in the middle of Sully's face.

"No," said Sully. "It's—"

"Blossom. Mr. ... uh ... B ..." Wippet scanned her class list to find Sully's name. "Mr. Brewster. Sullivan. I have a class to teach. Save your fraternizing for after class and turn your attention to Tennyson's 'Lady of Shalott.'"

Blossom winked at Sully as he gritted his teeth and clasped his hands tightly in front of him.

"Sorry about that, Mr. B. Wait. No," Blossom said, reconsidering. "Not Mr. B. Bee Boy. Yes, I like it. It has a nice ring to it."

Before turning to face the front, she wrapped her hands over his whitened knuckles and smiled.

"You're not actually my type. But I can tell we're going to be friends."

CHAPTER 9

"Come to our next class prepared to talk about what you think Tennyson is saying in this poem," Wippet said at the end of class. "Without giving too much away, I ask you to consider what the Lady's curse is. How does she see the world and what are the implications of that?"

Sully bolted for the door as soon as the bell rang, leaving room 211 and taking an uncustomary left turn. Morsixx had Sex Ed next period, meaning he'd be ascending the central stairway off the open atrium at the same time that Sully descended it. The easiest way to avoid him was to use the west stairwell, which Sully darted for now.

Dodger leaned casually against the west stairwell door frame and waggled his fingers at him, while hugging Sully's bag to his side.

"Give it back," said Sully.

"Give it back," Dodger mimicked, his voice pitched high and whiney.

Sully made a grab for it, but then saw Tank in the stairwell behind Dodger.

He stumbled backward and through the flow of students on his way to the east stairwell, but veered back to center when he saw that Ox blocked this alternate route.

Still bent on evading Morsixx, Sully shrank into himself, and joined the crowd that flowed down the broad central stairway like lemmings.

His timing was terrible. Halfway down, as the students in front of him began parting left and right, Sully found himself face to face with Morsixx. Well, almost face to face. Even one stair down, Morsixx was taller than Sully, and in a lucky break, he was looking at someone over Sully's shoulder.

Sully took a step to the left and made his way back up to the second floor. He stole slowly, keeping his head down and his shoulders braced, ready to slip away if Morsixx called his name.

He almost made it.

With his foot on the top step, plotting his escape down the right hallway, he heard his name shouted above the din.

"Hey, Sally, catch!"

Sully had just enough time to raise his hands before his backpack hurtled toward him.

"Whaddya know," said Dodger as he bumped past him. "This *is* your backpack after all!"

Sully staggered backward from the force and landed awkwardly. His unzipped backpack opened wide and spilled its contents down the now nearly empty middle of the stairway.

"Eww ... you're disgusting." This from a girl four steps down on his left.

"Perverted newb," said another girl.

"Hey, Booster!" catcalled a boy from his middle school. "Your time of month?"

"Taking your Sex Ed presentation a little too seriously, aren't you, kid?" said a boy from his Sex Ed class.

In the ensuing cacophony of whistles, laughter, and shouting, Sully scrambled to his knees and swiped at the surprising quantity of paraphernalia his bag had dumped in a strange swath down the stairs. As he shoveled things back into his pack, he searched through the blur of faces, and then looked back at his bag, as his scooping efforts met with abrupt resistance.

On the first-floor landing, Miss Winters stomped her

high heel on the end of a little white string, the other end of which was in Sully's hand.

"Mr. Brewster!" she said. "What is the meaning of this?"

Sully looked from the chilly sharpness of Winters's scowl to the tubular white item in the palm of his hand.

It was a tampon.

But not just one tampon. Looking from his hand to Winters's face, and then back again, Sully next let his eyes surf the trail that connected them. An alarming number of snow-white tampons were tied together, end to end, marking the middle of the stairway like the passing line on a highway.

"I ... I ... I—"

The area was silent in anticipation of Sully's explanation.

"I ... I—"

Winston emerged from the group. He walked up the stairway to where Sully stood and put his arm around him.

"I think it's pretty, Bella," he said. "They look like little sausages. Only white."

"The office, Mr. Brewster." Winters removed her foot from the little white string. "And bring your little art project with you. The rest of you, move along."

The rest of the students, most smirking, some scowling,

filed past Sully. Not one of them gifted him a scrap of privacy.

As Sully descended, scooping the tampons into his pack as he went, the only faces that didn't show ridicule were those of Morsixx and Blossom. They stood on opposite sides of the stairwell below him, like mismatched bookends, and shot him concerned and sympathetic glances.

Waiting in the hallway outside the principal's office, Sully noticed his reflection in the darkened glass.

His face had rearranged itself again.

CHAPTER 10

Correction. His face was in the process of rearranging. The scene in the dark glass of the office window played out like a macabre Shadow Play. Sully's eyes wobbled uncertainly up the left side of his face. As if to avoid a collision, his nose slid away from his encroaching eyes. It accelerated around his jawline like someone stealing home, and then wavered precariously on the tip of his chin.

Sully leapt to his feet. He placed his palms on the window and leaned closer to get a better look.

His eyes did a full revolution, in opposite directions, around the circumference of his face, before launching a two-pronged attack on his ear, which darted to his forehead. This caused a chain reaction that dislodged his mouth, which ricocheted off his hairline, before meandering sideways to rest vertically on his left cheek. Raising his eyeballs, now fixed one just above the other in the middle of his face, Sully watched his other ear slip from the top of his head and make a precipitous drop to the right side of his neck.

Sully raked his hair back from his scalp and pawed his face. Little strangled noises escaped his mouth. Which was now on his left cheek.

"Mr. Brewster." The principal's door swung inward, and Miss Winters ushered Sully inside. "This is not kindergarten. Stop making those ridiculous faces."

"But ... but ... but—"

"Speak up, young man. I'll need an explanation for that offensive spectacle on the stairwell."

"With respect, Ma'am," said a voice behind him. "The Dude was framed."

Sully spun to see Morsixx and Blossom approaching from behind.

"Most definitely framed," said Blossom, as she took a step toward the principal. "Another boy confiscated his backpack in Ms. Wippet's English class. He clearly spiked it with that ridiculous display."

"Is this true, Mr. Brewster?"

"Um ... yes?"

"Is that a question or an answer?" Winters arched an eyebrow.

"An answer, Ma'am?"

"And just who is this other boy who framed you?"

"I just joined the class today," said Blossom. "I don't know the other boy's name."

"Mr. Brewster?" Winters scrutinized his face.

"I ... it ... I—"

"Yes?" said Winters.

"I'd ... rather not say," he said.

"If you won't give me his name, I'll have to hold you responsible. I'd advise you to think a little harder."

"Well, I can point him out," said Blossom.

"No," said Sully. "I should have kept better track of my things. I don't want to get anyone else involved." The last thing he needed was to draw more attention to himself by tattling on one of Tank's lackeys.

Because his peripheral vision was severely compromised by the current location of his eyes— which crowded close to each other in the middle of his face—Sully had to turn his head to see the confused expressions Morsixx and Blossom gave each other.

"If that's the case," said Winters, "report to room 111 for a one-hour detention after school."

"Yes, Miss Winters." Sully rose and took the slip of paper Miss Winters handed to him.

Morsixx and Blossom opened a space between them to let Sully pass.

"What's up with that, Dude?" said Morsixx.

"That boy deserves to get in trouble!" said Blossom.

"Your inner Kermit, Dude," said Morsixx. "You're not going to solve your problems by hiding."

Sully disagreed. He pushed through the door of the school office and scanned the halls quickly from left to right, before galloping off without another word.

CHAPTER 11

The detention was a stroke of luck. Not that Sully had been discreet in ditching Morsixx, but this saved him doing it twice in one day. Of course, it meant he'd missed the bus home, but as he started out on foot, he realized this was way safer anyway. If he walked instead of busing it, he could evade everyone's attention entirely. Besides, he figured he could use the time to think.

The two-mile walk took Sully through Fairy Lake, an expansive park in the center of town. He cut across the south end through the boardwalk that followed the train tracks.

Hours of web searches hadn't coughed up any explanation for the state of his face. While it was distressing, at least no one else could see what he saw, and he had almost got used to looking at himself.

But now it had all changed again. Out of sight

of other people, he let his fingers explore the new configuration. His insides tumbled and turned as if they were rearranging, too, and heavy pressure sat vice-like at the top of his chest.

He veered along the path through the playground that would ultimately dump him onto True Street. A woman shuffled toward him with an enormous black purse slung over her shoulder. A weird sense of déjà vu swept over Sully and he almost stopped, when he noticed that the woman was making strange faces at him. First she'd rub her eyes and then stare at him, and then rub her eyes again and stare again. It was almost like a game of peekaboo, except really creepy.

Sully tugged his cap low over his face and ran past her. He sprinted a hundred yards before he stopped, breathing hard, and peeked behind him to see if she was still there.

She wasn't.

He slowed his breathing and tried to think clearly. All his googling had been regarding his face as a whole, but maybe he was approaching it all wrong. Nobody else could see what he saw. Maybe his face wasn't really rearranged at all. Maybe he was just having vision problems.

No, that's stupid, he thought. He could actually *feel* his nose in its new location on the tip of his chin. Besides, if it was his vision that was the problem, then everything would look weird, but the only thing that was messed up was his face.

"Whoa." Sully said this thought aloud. "Except that house."

True Street was hardly a street at all, considering it contained only a single house. A duplex squatted in the middle of the short block that faced the lake.

The two sides of the house were mirror opposites. At least they used to be. Sully hadn't walked here in a while, and the two sides were definitely more opposite than mirror now.

The stucco exterior on the left side emanated a tasteful pale yellow. The tidy black door demurely inspected the recently manicured, golf-green lawn. This side of the house said please and thank you and spoke in whispers.

Someone new must have moved into the right side, which shouted and lunged at the street. A seamless progression of purples vaulted the stucco walls, building from a soft mauve at the bottom to a garish, in-your-face violet at the top. The chimney bricks, painted alternately in bright shades of pink and orange, boasted a bold checkerboard motif, while the window frames provided a neon green accent.

That strange déjà vu feeling came over Sully again. Something about the purple stabbed him with remembered anxiety, as if it were the ugly bus ride on the first day of high school all over again.

It wasn't just the house that was strange. The wild and overgrown lawn, freckled with scruffy patches of thistle and ragweed, plotted escape from the snake-rail fence that corralled it. Affixed to the fence with twist ties and ribbon, possibly playing double duty to save the fence from collapsing, a parade of plastic figurines posed in random groupings.

Maybe there's something wrong with my eyes, after all, he thought. He certainly didn't remember the house looking like this.

Tearing his eyes from the obscenity of it all, he noticed a little Charlie Brown figurine on the fence post nearest him. The figurine's hands had been duct-taped to cover his face, which was missing its nose and half of its mouth. Pumbaa sat close at Charlie Brown's feet, the warthog's wide, flat features all soulful and innocent. Sleeping Beauty, with vines and flowers etched in felt marker on her colorful gown, and a Red Cross knight dressed in black armor and chainmail, were positioned in front of Charlie Brown. Small yellow roses had been attached with twist ties to their hands, which were thrust in Charlie Brown's direction. Darth Vader, flanked by Goyle and The Riddler, completed the circle around him.

Whoa, thought Sully. *Way too many universes colliding here. Disney*, Star Wars, *Harry Potter*, DC. *It looks like a mini Comic-Con Convention.*

Sully crossed to the lake side of the street and continued walking. He felt strangely better after seeing the purple house. It was like an advertisement for crazy. As confused as Sully felt, he knew he wasn't as messed up as whoever lived there.

A few more steps and he'd reach Perdu Avenue. From there it was only another five minutes home.

But he didn't make it that far.

CHAPTER 12

As Sully reached the dividing line between mellow yellow and violent violet, he pivoted slowly to the realization that he was being followed. At first, he expected to see the weird old lady with the purse, but the reality was worse. Tank leaned against a tree just yards away, while Dodger jumped around excitedly, and Ox repeatedly punched his right fist into the palm of his left hand.

Sully darted a look at the fence scene now on his right. There was nothing he wanted more at that moment than to cover his eyes like the Charlie Brown figurine, as if that could make the trio disappear. Because Tank, Ox, and Dodger definitely weren't offering flowers.

"Any cramping, Sally?" said Dodger. "Need any Midol?"

Sully swallowed hard. He forced himself to grin,

which tugged uncomfortably at the ear affixed to his forehead. Maybe if he acted casual and unfazed, they'd leave him alone.

"Heh heh ... good one. You got me there." He shuffled his right foot back and then his left, as if launching into a super-slow-motion moon walk. If he could reach Perdu without them noticing, he wouldn't be so isolated.

"You have a talent for stupid." Tank's bored eyes bored into Sully's own. "It must suck to be you."

"Yah, well, you know. I guess, yah ... pretty much." It did suck. Tank was right. Especially at that moment. Because what sucked most for Sully, as he listened to his own voice, was knowing what a suck he was being, and knowing he was too sucky to do anything about it.

"Bet you wish you could disappear sometimes," said Tank.

Sully nodded. Disappearing would be a fantastic trick right about then.

"Well." Sully jerked his head over his shoulder and twitched his thumb in the same direction. "I gotta get home. Yah. So. I gotta, like ... you know ... go."

"Don't want to worry Mommy?" said Dodger.

"What? No! Just ... you know ... homework to do."

"Oh, that's right," said Tank. "It's getting close to your time of the month to teach us about your ... time of the month."

Ox and Dodger snorted.

"Enjoying your research, Sally?" Tank said.

"Well, no, I ... I mean, you know, it's ... yah ... that is, no, I ... well, anyway. I'd better be going."

Sully wanted to punch himself to get it over with. Tank had asked him if he respected himself. He'd better start showing some self-respect.

He made himself stand up straighter and cleared his throat. He rolled back his shoulders and lifted his chin. Unconsciously replicating Tank's bored expression, he narrowed his eyes a little, which, considering their placement, didn't make him feel as cool as he'd hoped.

"Are you mocking me?" Tank pushed off from the tree and took a step toward Sully.

"What? No!" Sucky Sully was full force back in action. "Definitely no. No way. Anyway, like I said, I ... I gotta fly."

Too late he realized that Ox and Dodger had sidled around behind him. When he spun to face Perdu, he tripped over Ox's extended foot. Making a surprising arc through the air, he landed cheek first and swallowed a mouthful of dirt.

"Like you said," said Dodger. "You gotta fly."

"What, the—" Tank doubled over and held his ear.

"What's the matter?" asked Dodger.

"Something hit me in the ear." Tank righted himself and glared at Sully. "Did you throw a rock at me?"

"Who, me?" Sully pushed himself backward on his butt and spit out dirt.

"It came from over there." Ox pointed in a vague direction down True Street.

The vacant road offered no clues, but something had definitely hit Tank in the side of the head. They all looked down to see a hard, green fruit about the size of a golf ball at his feet. A walnut pod, Sully realized.

Sully seized the opportunity to stumble to his feet. Before he could slink away, he heard something connect with Tank's skull again, triggering an impressive string of unrepeatable words.

"What the—?" Dodger reached for the acorn-sized bump sprouting in the middle of Tank's forehead.

"Get off me." Tank shoved Dodger sideways.

"Did you throw this?" Ox picked up a second walnut pod at Tank's feet.

"What? Me?" Sully's backward steps were far less subtle this time. "I didn't throw it. I swear!"

Sully darted a look behind him to calculate how many steps he'd need to take before he could disappear around the corner onto Perdu. As he turned back to face Tank, he thought he saw something flash in the dormer window of the purple house. Ignoring it, he found his gaze involuntarily climbing Tank's forehead where the bump had doubled in size.

"What are you looking at?" said Tank.

"Nothing," said Sully. "I'm looking at nothing."

"Correction," said Tank. "*I'm* looking at nothing. *You* are nothing. *Less* than nothing. Get out of my sight."

Eager to do exactly this, Sully jogged backward a few feet as Ox and Dodger shifted awkwardly on either side of Tank.

"Tank, man, are you okay?" Dodger touched the spot on his own forehead where Tank's bump beamed an unflattering red.

"You got a problem?" Tank punched Dodger's hand away and narrowed his eyes.

"No problem, Tank." Dodger cradled his bruised hand.

"No problem," echoed Ox.

"Shoo, little Sally." Tank flicked his index finger as if Sully was a bug. "Send our regards to that Emo freak you're going steady with."

As Sully turned back to sprint home, the glint from the dormer flashed in his eyes again. A millisecond later, the right curtain panel fell back into place and fluttered a bit through the open window.

In front of which was a massive walnut tree.

CHAPTER 13

The stars were still visible when Sully set off for school on foot the next morning. Arriving a half hour before the bus, he cleared all his stuff out of the locker and left Morsixx a note:

I had a run-in with Tank yesterday and he mentioned your name. You need to stop the Morsixx stuff. You're practically begging for the Black Spot. Either way, I need to keep a low profile. The locker's yours till the whole Naked Niner thing is over.

Sully hoped Morty would heed the warning. While he had resolved to stay under Tank's radar until someone else was targeted, he didn't want it to be Morty. The poor guy was so self-unaware it was scary. His all-black clothes and skulls and chains clearly made him a target, but underneath it all, he was a good guy. Still, Sully had a feeling that all the bad luck he'd personally had since the school year began made him and Morty like Nitro and Glycerin. Steering clear of each other until after it was all over was doing them both a favor. Despite the fact that one of his eyes slid up to his forehead as he hid out in the boys' bathroom until the bell rang, Sully felt better than he had in weeks.

Until Blake Muir's presentation in Sex Ed.

Blake strode to the front of the class like an actor taking the stage.

"Hygiene, Gentlemen," Blake began. "Good diet. Lack of stress. These are your weapons against the cruel joke most of you are victims of: a.k.a. Acne Vulgaris."

Blake himself, with perfect hair and prep boy good looks, had a flawless and tanned complexion. No zit dared deface his perfect Greek God nose.

"Now, acne goes by many names," he continued. "Papules, pustules, nodules or, the more familiar, pimples and zits. But, to paraphrase Shakespeare, a zit by this or any other name will swell and secrete ..."

Blake paused here for effect. While his Shakespearian wordplay went over his classmates' heads, "pimples, papules, pustules, and zits" elicited the desired reaction.

"Will swell and secrete," he raised his voice over the groans, "because of a single underlying cause: oily build-up. Let me demonstrate with some lucky volunteers."

It was soon evident that this was to be no solo performance.

"You!" said Blake, pointing to a boy named Kyle at the back. "Show us Exhibit A."

Obviously prepped for the performance, Kyle jumped up and raced to the front like a contestant on a game show.

"Gentlemen," said Blake, handing Kyle a piece of Bristol board.

Kyle flipped the board over with Vanna White precision, cueing Blake to point to the oversized, disgusting image he'd pasted to the other side.

"Let me introduce you," Blake continued, "to the blackhead."

"Gil!" Blake called, pointing at another of his friends. "Show us Exhibit B."

Gil's sign had an equally nasty photo, this time of a whitehead.

"Gentlemen," said Blake, cuing up his PowerPoint presentation now. "Know it or not, these two odious specimens are members of what is called the Comedone family. Google it. Sounds like a mob family, right? And like the mob, the Comedones are stealthy and merciless, attacking when and where you least expect.

"Now, where do these nasty little explosions come from? Well, I have to warn you ... the conception of the common pimple is far less titillating than the conception of a human baby ... the topic my man Jason gets to present to you next Friday."

Blake pointed to a boy at the back who stood up, bowing to cheers and whistles.

With clever quips and an easy manner, Blake led the class through the causes and cures of acne.

"Now, Gentlemen," Blake said. He held up his hands to quiet the laughter and commentary. "We come to the family member no one wants to talk about. Help me out here, Brewster."

Tank walked casually into the classroom at this point. He tossed his bag from across the room before taking his seat.

"Nice interruption," said Green. "That'll be an extra ten laps before football practice after school. Continue, Mr. Muir."

Unfazed by the disturbance, Blake grabbed Sully's

arm and spun him out of his front row seat to face the class. As Sully regained his footing, Blake pushed another cardboard sign into his hand.

"The blind pimple." Blake shook his head in mock sorrow. "You know what I'm talking about. This is the guy who tries to hide in plain sight, pretending he's not there. But we know better, don't we. When this character shows up, the only one he's fooling is himself, right? I mean, you can't miss him. There he is, right in the middle of your chin ..." Blake thrust the pointer at Sully's chin, which hit his nose and caused him to sneeze.

"Or the middle of your forehead." Blake poked Sully in the eye this time. "He's red, he's sore, he's ugly ... no offense, Brewster ... but there's no easy way of getting rid of him. He's just gotta be exposed."

Tank stared unsmiling from the back row. The bump in the middle of his forehead lasered Sully like a third eye.

Sully tried to make himself as inconspicuous as it is possible to be, when posing as a blind pimple in front of a group of adolescent boys. He didn't take in much more of what Blake had to say about the root cause or remedy for blind pimples. He did, however, decide that humor might be the best defense for his own upcoming presentation.

He also made note of the fact that with Tank at football practice every day after school, he could now fearlessly walk home through the park.

Sully skulked out of Sex Ed only after he was sure Tank was long gone, and then sidled through the hallways via a circuitous route. He arrived late to English to find that Wippet had rearranged the desks in pairs, and that the only empty seat was next to the girl with the flower tattoos.

"There you are!" said Blossom as Sully took his seat.

"Hmph," said Sully.

He slouched sideways with his elbow on the desk between them.

Blossom was someone else he'd have to find a way to avoid. His gut told him that association with anyone peculiar that would draw unwanted attention to himself was a really bad idea until after the Naked Niner was over. Blossom definitely fell into that category.

"Good news," said Blossom. "You and I are partners for the term project."

"Hmph," said Sully, and then, "What?"

He turned to look at her as she held up a sheet of paper.

"Our comparative essay on 'The Lady of Shalott,'" she said. "I'm really excited about it. We have to compare

Tennyson's poem to a contemporary novel. There are so many possibilities!"

"I didn't choose you as a partner," said Sully.

"You were late," she said. "And stop being so rude, Bee Boy. You're lucky to have me as a partner, given that you don't look like much of a reader."

"I can read," said Sully.

"That's not what I meant," said Blossom. "Reading practically *is* my life. Trust me on this. We're going to do something fantastic."

"Great." Sully rolled his eyes, which made him a little nauseous given their current location.

"You're right," Blossom said, "it is great. Let's meet after school so we can get started."

"If you two are finished," said Wippet, nodding in Sully's direction, "can you tell me what the Lady is weaving in Tennyson's poem?"

Sully jerked back in his seat, looking hopefully around.

"Yes, you, Sullivan," Wippet continued. "Tell me what you think."

Sully stuttered a few incoherent words that raised giggles from his classmates.

"Quiet, class. We're all here to learn." Wippet nodded at Sully. "Please, Sullivan, continue."

"A tapestry?" said Sully.

"True on a literal level," said Wippet. "Anyone else?"

Relieved to be let off the hook, Sully relaxed back into his seat.

Beside him, Blossom sketched an intricate flower in brilliant shades on the inside of her arm. The lines from her pen flowed seamlessly from the other flowers and vines he'd previously presumed were permanent tattoos.

CHAPTER 14

Sully's fingers stumbled over Charlie Brown as he dragged his hand along the fence rail between True Street and Perdu Avenue. The little figurines had been repositioned along the weathered wood, or maybe the wind had just turned them. Charlie Brown's hands remained duct-taped to his face, and Pumbaa still crouched at his feet, but he now had his back to Sleeping Beauty and the Knight who, though still proffering flowers, were closer together and turned away from Darth Vader, Goyle, and The Riddler.

A fracture of sunlight blinked from near the roof the way it had the afternoon before. Sully's gaze galloped to the source in time to see a hand pull away from the curtains. Even closed, however, the cloth was flimsy enough to reveal the outline of a figure looking down at him.

Sully hauled his gaze back to the sidewalk. He suddenly felt a little like he was walking underwater, as he turned his body to the corner and willed his legs to carry him there. He could feel the eyes from the window watching his every move as closely as if they were glued to his back.

He dared a peek back at the purple house only after he'd reached the end of the street, and then chided himself for overreacting. Whoever lived there apparently had a wicked throwing arm, but with his or her fixation on little plastic toys, probably had the IQ of a squirrel.

There was only one other person on Perdu, a block up and on the opposite side. Sully put his head down and contemplated the sidewalk as he sorted through his thoughts. This walk would become tiresome in bad weather, but he'd only have to do it until mid-October. End of October at the latest. Just until Tank selected his victim.

It was only because of the eye sitting at the top of his forehead that Sully became aware that the person up ahead, a middle-aged woman, had crossed over to his side of the street. Now only yards away, she planted herself in the middle of the sidewalk and stared straight at him.

It was the woman with the purse.

Without missing a step, Sully veered off the sidewalk and crossed to the other side.

He'd only taken three steps, however, when she was on the move again. This time she crossed the road on a diagonal that would put them face to face within ten yards.

Sully stepped into the street on a ninety-degree angle to dodge their inevitable collision, but the woman turned then, too. She headed straight toward him until they came to a stop, face-to-face, in the middle of the road.

The Purse Lady stared unblinking and then leaned toward him and squinted. Sully shrunk back and sidled sideways to break their awkward encounter. Unabashed, the woman took another step toward him and then leaned slightly back herself, as if to get a better look.

She knit her brow and placed her hands on her hips.

As Sully took another step back, she bellowed, "Boy! What happened to your face?"

CHAPTER 15

Sully moved his mouth to say something, but all that came out was empty air. He watched as the woman placed her index fingers on the lids of her eyes and then traced a path around her face, coming to rest in the exact position in the middle of her face that Sully's own eyes currently inhabited.

She cocked her head to one side and then extended two fingers to within inches of his mouth, before sweeping them back to her own mouth and then to the left side of her face.

"What happened to your face?" she said again.

Before he could answer, something round and green rolled from across the street, and spun to a stop between them.

Sully looked in the direction it had come from, but there was no one there.

Or maybe there was. Something vaguely human-looking stood, barely visible, behind the stalks of ragweed. Sully squinted to get a better look, as a long metal stick dragged slowly out of view behind the weeds.

"Oh!" gasped the woman.

Sully turned back to find her reaching for something on the road between them. She stood slowly and studied the green ball she'd picked up. Another walnut pod.

She turned it over and over in her hand. She held it up at eye level as if she expected it to hatch or morph into something else. She breathed on it and polished it against her shoulder, even though the thick rind was coarse and nubbly.

Sully stepped sideways, away from her. Curious, he watched for a moment as she extracted a folded piece of paper from the big black purse that hung over her shoulder. With trembling fingers, she unfolded the paper and placed the fruit on top. The circular drawing in the middle of the page was a little smaller than the pod, and multi-colored, like a little rainbow.

"It's just a walnut pod," Sully offered. "And what did you mean about my face?"

She scared him a little. Maybe more than a little. But what *did* she mean about his face? If she could see what happened to him where no one else could, that seemed important.

The Purse Lady dropped the walnut pod and held the piece of paper against her chest, while staring at the air in front of her.

"Hello?" Sully said. "Tell me what you mean about my face."

She refolded the paper, tucked it carefully back in her purse, and then crossed to the sidewalk away from him, before plodding slowly back up the street the way she came.

CHAPTER 16

Out of the corner of his eyes, Sully saw something move along True Street. As he turned to look, the front door of the purple house swung shut. He picked up the walnut pod and closed his fist around it. A useful weapon if he were ever to need one.

Long after arriving home, he debated with himself about what he would do the next time he saw the Purse Lady, but his meditation was ambushed by a statement from Eva at dinner.

"I drew a picture in class today that the teacher liked," said Eva, "and Rooster did some art, too."

"Why, you're not even in Vanny's school, Princess," said Bill.

"My friend Jennifer's brother Nathan picked her up at school today and he told me."

"Sullivan?" said Mom.

"I have no idea what she's talking about," said Sully. Distracted by thoughts of the Purse Lady, he spilled peas from his fork as he pointed it to the side of his face.

"The dolls," said Eva. "The little white women."

"I got nothing," said Sully.

"Brewster," insisted Eva. "Nathan said so. The paper dolls. No. Not paper. Napkins, I think he said. He said even the Principal wanted to see it, and that I should let Mom and Dad know because you might be too shy. He said the whole school saw it. Good job, Brewster."

Fiery heat climbed from the nose on Sully's neck to the ear on top of his head, as it dawned on him what Eva was referring to.

"Sullivan?" Mom said again.

"Whoa," said Bill. "What's with the sudden sunburn, Vanny. Don't be embarrassed to share your good news."

"It's nothing," said Sully. "Nathan was just making a joke. It wasn't even my work."

"Don't be modest," said Bill.

"Yes," agreed Eva. "Don't be modest. Nathan said you made it. The little women made of napkins that floated down the school stairs."

Bill gave Sully a confused look as he fumbled through a modified version of the little white sausages.

Eva frowned in disappointment while Mom looked more than a little skeptical.

"Is everything okay at school, Sullivan?"

"It's great," said Sully. "Everything is great."

Mom still didn't look convinced, but she let it ride.

"Okay, then," she said. "So, tell us about your picture, then, Eva. What did you draw?"

As uncomfortable as this exchange was, it gave Sully an idea for his presentation, which was only a few days away.

Eleven days.

And thirteen hours.

Blake had used what Wippet called "allegory." Or was it "metaphor?" Whatever. Blake had set up the different kinds of acne as various members of a Mob family. Maybe Sully could do the same, so he'd never actually have to talk directly about his topic at all.

He knew an allegory was telling a story that had a hidden meaning. He remembered learning that even the Narnia story wasn't really about lions and witches and children, and all those other things that were half-man and half-animal. Well, it wasn't only about that. Well, perfect. Hiding his subject was exactly what he intended to do.

With a sketchy outline chasing itself in circles in the back of his head, Sully began framing a comic strip about some pale white women warriors parting ... no, better yet, stopping the Red Sea. That was in the Bible, right? And wasn't there something about a baby floating down a river in a basket? He wasn't at all sure one had anything to do with the other, but at least it was a start, and he had to weave in the whole baby reference somehow. As in, because of the flood, there would be no baby. He could tell a story about little crusaders in little boats stopping a flood. Wow, another biblical reference. Noah and the flood. And wasn't the flood forty days and forty nights? He was pretty sure a menstruation cycle lasted something like that long. It was so perfect, he couldn't believe someone hadn't thought of it before.

Within half an hour, he'd invented the whole presentation, and not once did he have to use any embarrassing words.

CHAPTER 17

There was no good place to hide out at lunch. If pretending to be a blind pimple in front of his Sex Ed class was humiliating, sitting alone in the cafeteria was just as bad. In fact, sitting alone anywhere was a bad option.

As he stepped into the fall sunshine, surrounded by random groupings of fellow students, Sully spied Morsixx and Blossom deep in conversation by one of the school pillars. Panicking, he launched himself into the parking lot and crouched behind a blue van.

As luck would have it, no sooner had he unwrapped his sandwich than a burly twelfth grader approached, keys in hand, and headed unmistakeably for the driver's door.

Sully dropped half his sandwich in his haste to clear out. He snuck around the back of the next car, looked both ways, and then slid in between a white sedan and a green station wagon, one row back. Feeling exposed between these two shorter vehicles, he slid to sitting and unwrapped the remaining half of his sandwich.

Without warning, the station wagon thrummed to life and pulled away, leaving Sully out in the open with his sandwich halfway to his mouth.

He scrunched his sandwich back in his bag and lit off for the second row at the end, where he wedged himself between a black pickup and a red Hummer. As he finally sank his teeth into the remaining half of a disappointingly dry tuna fish sandwich, Sully squealed when a hand landed on him from behind.

"I found you, Bella!"

"Winston! You scared me to death! Don't sneak up on people like that."

"I found you! I found you!" Winston laughed giddily. "My turn!"

As Winston jumped up and down, rubbing his palms together, a girl jumped into the black pickup seconds before Sully's history teacher, Mr. Escrow, walked up to the Hummer.

"We're playing hide and seek!" Winston said to Escrow. He raised his hand for a high five.

"I can think of safer places for games." Escrow tagged

Winston's hand but gave Sully a stern look.

"But we're not really playing hide and seek," said Sully. "I was just—"

"Whatever you're doing, I think it might be better to move the game to the field," said Escrow. "Don't you think?"

"Bye, Mister!" Winston patted the Hummer and waved as Escrow pulled away.

Completely visible now to the front of the school, Sully took the opportunity, when Winston's back was turned, to flee around the back of a beat-up van a row back.

"Bella?" Winston yelled. "Bella, where are you? It's my turn to hide!"

Sully poked his head out so Winston could see him and put his finger to his lips. Which were still sideways on his left cheek.

"I'm not playing hide and seek, Winston," he whispered. "You should go."

"You can't fool me, Bella," Winston said loudly and grinned. "I've been watching you! Start counting!"

"I'm not kidding, Winston." Sully whispered louder this time. He gave Winston an angry look so he'd get the point, and as he did so, his nose back-flipped to the top of his head and his ears swiveled in opposite circles, landing on either side of his jaw. But backward. "Please go! And my name's not Bella."

"Is it Isabella?" Winston looked puzzled. "Elizabella? No ... Elizabella's not a name. Annabella?"

The van roared to life in front of him and eased out of the parking space to avoid Winston—which left Sully out in the open again. Aware that a few of the students in front of the school were catching on to the commotion, Sully dropped to all fours and crawled behind a yellow Prius one space over.

"Oh, oh, oh! I know ... Bellatrix!" yelled Winston. "Hey, where'd you go, Bella?"

"Stop calling me that. It's Sully," whispered Sully. He poked his head out and put his finger to his lips again, as they toppled sideways, now upside down, into the middle of his face.

"It's not silly, Bella." Winston smiled again. "Bella's a pretty name. Count to ten, Bella, and then find me!"

"I'm not counting to anything, Winston. Just leave me alone."

"But it's my turn." Winston's grin wobbled as he cocked his head to one side. "You have to take turns."

"I'm not playing some stupid game," Sully said.

As he ducked behind the Prius again, the eye on his

forehead shifted center in Cyclops fashion, while his other slipped down to the middle of his chin.

"Oh," said Winston. He scrunched his eyes closed and covered his ears. "Stupid's not a nice word, Bella."

"I just don't want to play." Sully shouted the words just as the yellow Prius shifted into drive and pulled away. Once again, Sully found himself on all fours in the middle of the parking lot.

Two cars in the first row and one in the second also took this opportunity to exit, so when Sully looked up, it was into the eyes of a dozen students who now had an unobstructed view of the proceedings.

"Hey, it's the tampon kid!" someone yelled.

Winston uncovered his ears at the crescendo of laughter and broke into an ear-splitting grin himself.

"You look kind of silly down there, Bella," he said. "And now I know why you don't want to play."

"What?" said Sully. "Why?"

Sully struggled to his feet. Across the parking lot, Morsixx and Blossom watched him from one side of the front steps. Tank, Ox, and Dodger eyed him from the opposite side.

"I'm sorry to say this, Bella," Winston said. "But you're really not very good at hiding."

CHAPTER 18

Sully's new nickname not only spread through the student body like a wave at a football game, it was also quickly spun off into a number of iterations. The Tampon Kid became, variously, Sanitary Man, Pad Man, guyPad, or, more simply, TK.

After a second reprimand by Escrow about playing in the parking lot kept him past the bell after school, Sully raced outside to begin his walk home. He spied Morsixx and Blossom at the bus stop just yards away. To avoid them, he slunk to the stoplights and ducked behind a kid named Ned, who played offensive tackle on the school's football team.

Friday afternoon. Two and a half days before he'd have to deal with any of this, he thought. He took a deep breath and could feel the tension begin to release from his body, until the thought occurred to him that Ned should be at football practice. He shouldn't be *here*.

"He-e-y, TK!" The wide receiver came up behind him. He grabbed Sully in a headlock and gave him a nuggy.

Neither the offensive tackle *nor* the wide receiver should be here.

Given the fact that Sully's nose was still on the top of his head, the wide receiver's rough knuckles incited a nosebleed which, in turn, roused a burst of laughter from the arriving quarterback.

"Yo, guyPad's bleeding!" said Ned.

"Don't you guys have practice after school?"

"Got any more supplies in your backpack?" said the wide receiver.

"Never known a niner with such a death wish," said the quarterback.

The trio greeted another player and seemed to forget about Sully.

He tried again. "No practice today?" Sully could put up with some stupid jokes and harmless ribbing in return for the answer to his burning question.

"It's Friday, little man," said Ned. "No practice on Friday. Hey, you'd better get home and rest up for however else you plan to sabotage yourself next week."

The wide receiver gave him another nuggy.

Sully spied the back of Tank getting on the bus. Mustering his limited athletic skills, he jogged, trotted, panted, and gasped his way home, until the park dumped him onto True Street. As he paused to catch his breath, his eyes ping-ponged between the dormer window and the crazy fence. It was only when he stood facing the large picture window that he noticed a shadowed figure behind the sheers. The hunched outline looked vaguely ape-like, if slight, but there was no mistaking that it was staring straight at him. Even through the curtains, its large eyes actually glowed.

Sully dropped his gaze to his feet to avoid any kind of eye contact. He noticed that one of the plastic figurines had been demoted to the bottom rail. Charlie Brown was now lying on its back a few feet from a plastic Madonna—the religious figure, not the singer. Madonna had a tiny hole through her chest where her heart would be, and a black backpack glued to her back.

It crossed Sully's mind that the wind couldn't have rearranged the figurines this time. Squirrel IQ or not, whoever lived in the purple house was seriously creepy. What was up with this rail-post storytelling, anyway?

Sully wasn't about to stick around to find out.

As the shadowed figure in the window moved toward

the front door, Sully sprinted forward, while keeping an eye on the purple house. He'd run further today than he'd probably run in the entire first thirteen years of his life, but this thought jarred out of his head when he collided with something at the corner of True and Perdu.

Prostrate on the sidewalk, Sully held his head as he propped himself up on one elbow. The woman with the purse looked down at him.

"While you're down there," she said, "can you look down the grate for me? My knees aren't what they used to be."

"You!" Sully said. "I need to talk to you."

"The sewer grate. There." The woman pointed to the road beside Sully's head. "I have a flashlight."

She dug inside her purse until she pulled out a flashlight.

"What did you mean by what you said yesterday?" Sully said.

"You look different today." She tapped her fingers on her forehead and her chin in the exact placement of Sully's eyes.

"Yah, like that," he said. "Tell me what you see."

"I'll tell you what I *don't* see." She held the flashlight out to him again. "I *don't* see what I'm looking for because

I *don't* see as well as I used to. And I *don't* see you trying to help me when I asked for your help."

"You asked me what happened to my face. What did you mean by that?"

"You don't know what your face looks like?" she said.

"*I* know what I look like," Sully said, "but no one else seems to see what I see."

"Everything's opposite in a mirror," she said. "You can't really see yourself the way others do."

"That's not what I mean," said Sully. "What I mean is that others can't see me the way I see myself."

"What's the difference?" she said. "You just said the same thing, except backward."

"Look, can you see my face ... *really* see my face?"

"That depends," said the lady. "Is that really what you look like or not?"

"Just tell me what you see," said Sully.

"I see what you see," she said.

"Which is what, exactly?"

"Your face."

"But is it normal?"

"Define normal."

"Look, you're the one who brought it up. You *stalked* me to ask what happened to my face."

"Well, what *did* happen to your face?"

"I don't know! That's what I'm trying to find out!"

"Well, how am I supposed to know what happened to you? I wouldn't have asked you the question if I knew the answer."

She lifted the flashlight between them again, using it to point at the sewer grate.

"Never mind." Sully waved the flashlight away.

"I don't see why you're so upset."

Sully shook his head. He *was* upset. Upset that he'd thought this crazy old lady might actually be able to help him.

"I'm not crazy," the woman said. "And I'm not that old."

"What?" Sully knew he hadn't said this out loud.

"Do you remember what it looks like?" She rummaged in her purse. "I can show you the picture again."

Another walnut pod rolled across the street to land between them again. Sully looked toward the purple house, but there was no one in sight.

"No," said the Purse Lady. She held out the flashlight again and pushed the walnut pod away with her foot. "That's not it. I thought you realized that yesterday."

Sully pushed the flashlight away again and frowned.

"An upside-down frown is a smile," she said.

"Go tell Facebook."

"What's face book?" She touched her own face and cocked her head to one side.

"Look," he said. "I made a mistake. Sorry I can't help you. I gotta go."

Reaching the corner of his street, he looked back once to see the woman, bent and focused, beaming her flashlight through the sewer grates.

Much later that evening, Sully woke from a restless sleep.

Wait, he thought. My mouth *is* upside down. And I *was* frowning. She really *can* see me.

CHAPTER 19

Dense clouds darkened Sully's path to school early Monday morning. Morsixx had called him seven times over the weekend. The guy just didn't get it.

Stepping carefully in the unnatural dark, Sully held onto the fence as he turned onto True Street. He half-hoped the crazy lady with the Mary Poppins purse might still be casing the sewer, so he could talk to her. She was definitely crazy, but he had a feeling if he could figure out how to ask the questions in the right way, she might have some answers for him.

Thunder rumbled in the distance, threatening rain. Sully let his hand glide along the fence. The figurines were indistinguishable blobs in the low light. He squinted through the muddy dawn at the strange house.

A tiny light pulled his eyes back to the fence. It bounced across the yard as if on a mission and made freaky ghoulish shadows of the man-high weeds.

Glued to the spot, Sully watched what he realized was a lantern float toward him about four feet off the ground. Suddenly it dipped down and stopped, resting between the fence rails, not two feet from where he stood.

Sully took a half-step back and froze again when a small sound reached him.

"Ah."

Sully made himself as small as possible. Had he been spotted?

"I see."

The voice was low and raspy. Sully had no intention of sticking around to see who or what had spoken these words.

But as he turned to bolt, something cold and dry like tree bark landed on his wrist. It held him in place with a scaly grip.

"Let me go!" Sully's plea tripped over three octaves. He yanked himself free, only to fall into the fence, which unbalanced the lantern. In the sweeping brightness, discs of light blinked on and off beside him like Morse code.

Blinded briefly by brightness as the lantern rocked to a stop in front of his face, Sully shrieked as a rod of glinting steel shot out. It hooked him under his right armpit and pinned him to the fence. As he struggled to detach himself, a scabby hand jammed his head against the fence rail, pressing his cheek against one of the figurines.

A crack of lightning ripped the sky. It illuminated the yard only briefly, but long enough for Sully to register a shrunken, hideous face mere inches from his own, with bulbous eyes too large to be human.

CHAPTER 20

In the darkness that followed the flash, the metal rod pinioning Sully's right shoulder released. It hooked the lantern and brought it up to Sully's face.

"My, my," the creature wheezed.

"Get away from me!" Sully yelled. "Help!"

"It changes things that you are here." The creature's voice, ancient as a mountain, rolled over Sully's ear like a hand dragged through gravel.

"Help!"

"It will happen as it happens." It loosened the pressure on Sully's head. "I see what I see, and that is all ... but I do what I can."

Sully's eyes adjusted somewhat to the dark. The creature raised spindly arms of steel, as if they were wings, and tipped its yellowed skull to the sky.

Sully lurched back. He threw his arms over his

face to shield himself from whatever new horror the creature was unleashing.

"Enough," it croaked, and maybe it was coincidence that, at this exact second, the thunder cut off mid-rumble. In the sudden silence, the dark skies parted, yanked like curtains to reveal a warm pink dawn beneath.

"Now," said the creature as it lowered its arms. "You'll be late for school. You'd best be going."

"Wait ... what?" Sully uncovered his eyes. He looked at the creature for the first time in full light.

Hunched over, its spine curved like a comma, the creature was not a creature at all, but a very old man. Dressed in beige trousers and a short-sleeved white shirt, his gnarled hands clutched two metal canes. Thick black-rimmed glasses wrapped his bald head aviator-style. Inch-thick lenses magnified each of his eyes to three times its size.

"Ah," said the man, "that will not do."

He reached out and plucked the little figurine still clinging to the side of Sully's face.

"That is ironic, to be sure." He held the little Charlie Brown figurine between them and surveyed the fence. "This is you. And this," he said, indicating the other figurines, "is your life. As it might be. As I see it."

Sully rubbed his cheek. His open mouth gaped in the middle of his face.

"You're not a monster." This was the most pressing thing. He had no idea what the man meant by the fence and his life.

"And *you're* not a vandal," said the man. "But you should still be careful about creeping around in the dark."

"I wasn't—"

"You're not as invisible as you think," the old man said.

"And you're not as frail as you look." Sully rubbed the spot on his head that had so recently been pinned to the fence.

"Neither are you," said the man.

Sully looked over the man's shoulder at the walnut tree.

"Are you the one who's been throwing those walnut things?"

"Do I look athletic to you?" The man held up his canes.

"Well, no, not athletic, but—"

"You think I could knock out a thug from a hundred yards?"

"I never said anything about knocking out a thug. But if you didn't knock out the thug, how do you know about it?"

"I have eyes, don't I?" said the man.

He definitely had eyes.

"That's not what I asked," said Sully.

The old man pursed his lips.

He totally threw those walnut things, thought Sully.

"I see lots of things," said the man.

"What about me?" said Sully.

It occurred to him that if the strange old lady could see his face, maybe the strange old man could, too.

"What *about* you?" said the man.

"Do you notice anything different about me?"

"It works best when I don't know too much about you," said the man.

"What works best?"

"The universe. Fate. Life. Luck. Will. Destiny. The whole kit and caboodle."

"Oh-h-h-kay." Sully darted a look at the fence. Definitely senile. Either that or the old man's been playing with dolls for too long.

"Don't judge what you don't understand." The man reaffixed Charlie Brown to the fence.

Sully wondered if the old man had just read his mind. "It's *your* fence," he said.

"It is my fence." The man nodded. "And it's best that I don't know your name. But you can call *me* Mr. C."

"Mr. C?" said Sully. "Like the letter?"

Mr. C. winked. He inscribed a semi-circle in the air that followed the crooked line of his body. "That's one way to look at it." His pupil loomed enormous as his eye re-opened and his lips parted in what might have been a smile.

"Why do you tie all those—?"

"I don't make the future, if that's what you think."

"That definitely wasn't what I was thinking."

"I just report what I see and make predictions. But every decision you make bends the story. You're the one in control, not me."

"In control? Of the story?" Sully looked at him blankly. "What is it I'm supposed to be in control—"

"So far, you're not doing so well." Mr. C. said this last part in a whisper as he cupped his voice with a crooked hand.

"Excuse me?"

"You should pay a little more attention to these two," Mr. C. whispered these words, too. As if nervous that someone would see him, he brushed his fingers across Sleeping Beauty and the knight with an exaggerated casualness, and then glanced self-consciously up at the rising sun.

"Never mind." Mr. C. took a step back and straightened his back to the extent he could. "That's your job to figure out. I don't want to jinx it."

"Jinx *what*?" said Sully.

"It is possible you're entirely beyond help." No whispering this time. Mr. C.'s lips were taut as he shook his head. "Now, you'd better be going. You may have to run to make it."

"How do you even know where I'm going? Is that one of your fencepost predictions?"

"You're a boy, aren't you?" said Mr. C. "Boys go to school in the daytime."

"Oh," said Sully. "Right. It's just that—"

"You overthink things," said Mr. C. "Sometimes the answer's as plain as the nose on your face."

"Right," said Sully. Which might explain why he was having so much trouble these days.

"So run, already," said Mr. C. With his back now to Sully, he hobbled toward the house. His canes lent him a ponderous, elephantine gait, like a second set of legs.

CHAPTER 21

Sully arrived at school out of breath and soaked with sweat. Skulking up to the second-floor bathroom, he grabbed a fistful of paper towels and mopped at the random placement of his face.

Focused as he'd been on catching his next breath, he hadn't had time to give Mr. C. much thought during his sprint to school. But now, strange flashes of their encounter left him with a thousand questions.

Before he could answer any of them, the bathroom door pushed inward. Sully yanked his focus back. His heart hammered as Tank sauntered in and leaned casually against the side wall. He lit up a cigarette and blew smoke in Sully's face, then cracked just the hint of a smile, as if not at all surprised to find Sully in here. Like a beacon, the now phlegm-green bump on Tank's forehead alerted Sully to impending disaster.

Sully's eyes started to water and his mouth went dry. For a panicked second, he grabbed desperately at the possibility that if he pretended not to notice Tank, maybe Tank would stop noticing him. He worked hard at not coughing or making any noticeable movements.

As he plotted the shortest space to the door, it swung inward again and spilled Ox and Dodger into the tiny space.

"Ha, ha, you were right, Tank," said Dodger. "Sally seems to have wet himself."

"It's just sweat," Sully said. "I—"

"Lot of paper towels there," said Dodger. "Have a little accident, did we?"

"I gotta get to class." Sully eyed the sliver of space between them.

"Well, we don't want to hang you up, Sally," said Dodger.

"Actually," said Ox, who grabbed the back of Sully's shirt, "yes, we do."

As Ox pushed Sully's skull into the back of the handicap bathroom stall, Dodger moved in from the side and yanked Sully's underwear halfway up his back. Together they looped the painfully stretched leg hole over the clothes hook and stood back to admire their handiwork.

Sully flailed like a marionette. He reached behind and tried to unhitch himself. Dodger convulsed with laughter, and Ox looked at Tank for approval.

"See you in class." Tank blew a lazy stream of smoke in Sully's face and led the duo out the door.

Sully arched his back in an effort to swing the door inward. If he could get his feet on top of the toilet seat, he might gain some leverage to loosen himself. The door swung back instead of forward, and the motion caused considerable pain to body parts that were already in distress.

Still, he either had to find a way out of this himself or suffer further embarrassment at the hands of anyone else who happened to walk in.

Which Morsixx did at that very moment.

"Oh, Dude." Morsixx shook his head. "That's nasty."

"Leave me alone," said Sully. "I can handle this by myself."

"Yah, looks like you're doing a great job of that. How long you been hanging out here, Dude? Never mind. You need my help, so just suck it up."

"Didn't you read my note?" said Sully.

"Yah, Dude, thanks for the warning. Maybe you should have written one to yourself, too. Here, push yourself up on my hand and use my shoulders to ease yourself off. I'm hurting just looking at you."

"I don't want anyone to see us in here together," said Sully. "If we're going to do this, make it fast."

Morsixx held his cupped hands steady, but the back of Sully's underwear didn't give up the hook easily. When it finally released, it did so all of a sudden, jolting Sully forward, which caused Morsixx to stagger back.

"Hold still, Morsixx!"

"You think I'm trying to dance here, Dude? Get a hold of yourself."

Sully grabbed wildly to stall his fall, clinging to Morsixx in the process, with his arms around his head and his legs around his chest.

"Morsixx! Let go of me! Put me down!"

"I'm not the one holding on, Dude. You're going to take us both down."

"Hold steady!"

"Let go!"

The two of them landed hard on the bathroom floor, face-to-face, Sully spread-eagled and flailing while Morsixx rolled out from under him.

"You nearly killed me." Sully bounced to his feet and looked around, as if witnesses might pop out of thin air.

"You're welcome," said Morsixx.

"We can't let anyone see us." Sully shut himself in a stall to undo the damage the wedgie had caused.

"I'm late for class." Sully exited the stall and headed for the door to the hallway. "Wait five minutes after I go before you leave."

"Say what?" said Morsixx.

"Look," said Sully. "Thank you for helping me, but the last thing I can afford is for someone to see us coming out of here together."

"Dude, you should be more afraid of being seen with yourself. Take a good long look in the mirror. You are so messed up these days."

"What are you saying?" said Sully. "What do you know about that?"

"Dude, look at yourself. Seriously."

Sully swung round to look at himself in the mirror. Pieces of him were chasing themselves around his face like a game of Pac Mac. His eyes were doing loop the loops, jockeying for position with his spinning ears and ping-ponging nose. His mouth yawned cavernously as if ready to swallow the whole lot.

A sharp rap on the bathroom door froze his features in their new location, all bunched together in the middle of his face, with one eye in each ear canal flanked by his lips and flaring nostrils.

"We're coming in!" It was Winters's voice. "Don't think I don't know what that odor is. I can smell it out in the hallway."

The door pushed inward as Mr. Caradine, the caretaker, paved the way for Winters.

"Coast is clear, Miss Winters," he said. "It's okay to come in."

"Has one of you been smoking?" Winters looked at Sully. "The penalty is suspension, but if you lie on top of that, you'll be expelled."

"It wasn't me!" said Sully.

"It wasn't either of us," said Morsixx.

"And yet, the evidence is evident," said Winters, sniffing the air. "Another student advised you were in here."

"There must've been dozens of students through here this morning," said Morsixx.

"That may be so," said Winters, "but that doesn't explain why you're hanging out in the boys' bathroom when you're supposed to be in class. I suppose it's just coincidence that you two are in here together at the exact same time? I know you're friends."

"Who says we're friends," said Sully.

"Whoa, Dude, that's harsh. You're even more messed up than I thought. My friend's just having a major identity crisis, Ma'am, but I—"

"*I'm* having an identity crisis?" said Sully. "Look who's talking. If anyone's having an identity crisis, Morsixx, it's you with your stupid Emo clothing!"

Morsixx ignored him and turned back to Winters.

"I'm telling you the truth. Neither of us is responsible for the cigarette smoke in here. The Dude was roughed up by some punks and I was helping him. That's all."

"Bullying?" said Winters. "We have zero tolerance for bullying at this institution. Who was bullying you, Mr. Brewster?"

"No one," said Sully. "I just tripped, Miss Winters."

"Pretty impressive trip," said Morsixx under his breath.

"You can talk to me," said Winters.

"Thank you," said Sully, "but I'm fine."

"Is everything okay, Miss Winters?" Dodger stood outside the door as the four of them walked out. "I was excused from class to use the washroom. Is it safe to use?"

"There's nothing to worry about, young man," Winters patted his shoulder and nodded. "Thank you for asking. Hurry along so you can get back to class."

"Oh, I will, Miss Winters." Dodger winked at Sully. He held up his phone behind the principal's back and swiped quickly through some photos Sully couldn't make out. "I made sure to time things so I wouldn't miss a thing."

CHAPTER 22

"Just in time, Brewster."

Some guy named Owen Black was in the midst of a presentation on gonorrhea when Sully walked in with a late slip. Owen's wide Grinch grin slid in place as he stepped in front of Sully and steered him to the front of the class.

"You decide to saunter in late to this class," said Green, responding to the look of protest on Sully's face, "you suffer the consequences. Proceed, Mr. Black."

"As I was saying, you have to be careful when courting the ... *lay-dies*." He said the word "ladies" in a high voice, with an exaggerated hand flourish toward Sully.

"Oh, wait ..." said Owen, as Sully batted his hand away. "My mistake. Geez, get a haircut, Brewster."

Everyone laughed as Sully pulled away and took his seat. Except Tank, whose smirk emitted something darker than simple amusement.

Bolting from Sex Ed as soon as the bell rang, Sully took refuge in English and ignored Dodger's sneer as he entered the classroom. Blossom, on the other hand, slipped into the classroom twenty minutes after the bell. She placed her late slip on Wippet's desk and walked to her seat as if navigating a narrow hallway.

"What'd you do?" said a girl as Blossom walked by. "Walk into a door or something?"

"Do you seriously think you look good?" said the girl in the desk beside her.

Blossom ignored them. She opened her book to a random page and stared straight ahead. Sully noted that she'd outlined her eyes in red and painted daffodils on her right cheekbone against a smear of purples and greens.

"We're going to use *The Handmaid's Tale* as our comparative novel," Blossom whispered, as Wippet turned to the blackboard and began writing notes she had instructed the class to copy down.

For a moment, Sully wondered if Blossom was even talking to him. She focused alternately between the blackboard and an elaborate doodle she was penning in the margin of her notes.

"What?" he whispered back, after a pause.

"It's a good fit," she said, still not looking at him. "Both heroines are imprisoned. Both struggle within a world of someone else's making. It doesn't matter if you haven't read it, because I have."

"Are you talking to me?" Sully leaned forward to peer into her face, which was turned slightly away from him.

She turned to look at him. The violets on her forehead overlapped each other as her brow creased.

"Never mind." While Blossom's dismissal was whispered, Sully felt the sting of it.

"Who appointed you Queen?" he said. "What are you, some kind of control freak?"

"Do you have another title in mind?"

"Another title?"

"A different book." She enunciated each word. "Do you have a different book you think would be better?"

"Well, no, I—"

"I thought not." She turned to face the board again. "If you want to think of something better, I'm all ears. One way or another, we need to get started."

"The maid thing's probably fine," said Sully. "What's it about?"

The violets criss-crossed her forehead again.

"It would probably be a good idea for you to at least get the title right."

"You do realize I'm in the middle of teaching this class, don't you?" Wippet had somehow approached the side of Sully's desk without him noticing.

"Talking in class is fine as long as it's on topic," Wippet continued. "So, let's put your verbosity to good use. Follow me."

Red-faced, Sully followed Wippet to the front of the class where she laid her volume of Tennyson's poetry open on his palms.

"Read from here," she said, pointing. "This will help you, Sullivan."

Sully raised the book to block the mocking faces of his classmates.

"But in her web she ... still delights to ... weave the mirror's magic sights for often thro ... thro ... like throw?" Sully looked to Wippet for direction.

"Like 'through,' Sullivan," Wippet supplied. "For often *through* the silent nights. Continue."

"For often through the silent nights ... a funeral with plumes ..."

"A funeral," interrupted Wippet, "and then you pause. Feel the syntax, Sullivan. Feel the words. A *funeral* went to Camelot. A funeral with plumes, which are feathers, and with lights and music. Try again."

"A funeral," said Sully, increasingly confused, "with plumes and lights and music, went to Camelot."

Sully paused and looked hopefully at Wippet.

"Try one more stanza and then you can take your seat."

Sully hid his face behind the book once more, and read, "Or when the moon was overhead came two young ... lovers lately wed—"

"Here it is," said Wippet. She closed her eyes and flung one arm out dramatically, while waving her other for Sully to continue.

"'I am half sick of shadows,' said the Lady of Shalott."

"Thank you, Sullivan. Thank you," said Wippet, taking the book from him. "You did just fine. It's a lovely phrase, isn't it?"

Sully shrugged.

"I am half sick of shadows, class," she repeated theatrically and nodded for Sully to take his seat. "Do you see? Suddenly we are out of the lady's web and into her head. 'I am half sick of shadows.' Tell me. What is she saying? What is the lady's heartache? What is she pining for?"

Sully slouched in his seat with his arms crossed. He pivoted away from Blossom and scowled against her expected criticism.

"Well, aren't you going to say something?" he said after a minute.

"Pardon?" She dragged her eyes off her notebook as if waking from a trance.

"Go ahead. Say what you're going to say."

"I am half sick of shadows," she said, but her gaze fell short of him.

"Whatever." Sully turned away again, but not before he saw that the intricate flowers in the margins of Blossom's notebook were not entirely random doodles. The layers of vine that connected one flower to the next were wound around the figure of a sleeping girl, spun up and bound like a fly in a spider's web.

CHAPTER 23

The day's events—the wedgie, Blossom's strange behavior, an unwanted stab of guilt when he thought of Morsixx—had pushed Mr. C. from Sully's head. As he approached the purple house on his way home from school, the morning's odd encounter with the old man rushed back.

Did he actually say the fence had something to do with Sully's life? That was kind of creepy, or maybe just sad. Or funny. Sully was pretty sure Mr. C. was senile, but there was a strange intrigue about him at the same time ... somewhere between crazy, awe inspiring, and cool.

Changes in the fence revealed the old man had been busy. Charlie Brown stood even further from the other figurines now. Still on the lowest fence post, he was side by side with Madonna, both of whom faced a shiny piece of tin foil that distorted their reflections.

Charlie Brown and Madonna. Sully smirked at the

ridiculousness of these two characters together. Mr. C. called it a prediction. Yah, right. In what universe?

In an exact reversal of the morning, Sully loitered outside the house, half hoping to talk to the old man. Instead, he almost bumped into the Purse Lady.

"Well, that's not good," she said.

"You can see how messed up my face is," Sully blurted. "Can't you."

"This arrangement is challenging to be sure." She scrutinized Sully's face as she inscribed a circle with her index finger around her own. "All the more reason you need to watch where you're going."

"Why can you see my face when no one else can?"

"If you want people to see your face, you should cut your hair."

"That's not what I mean, and you know it. I mean *this*." He grabbed his jaw for emphasis. "How messed up I am. You can see it. I know you can."

"A little give and take," she said.

"What?"

"You have to give a little to get a little."

"What does that even have to do with what we're talking about?"

"It's just this." She rummaged in her purse, pulled

out a pair of mismatched socks, and tucked them under her arm.

"No," she said. "Not that. Give me a minute."

After the socks, she pulled out a half-eaten muffin, some pliers, a deck of cards, a paperback book, a tin of tuna, some newspaper, a roll of toilet paper, a bag of buttons, some knee-highs, and a blanket.

Sully gawked. It seemed impossible that she could fit all this and more into her purse. It wasn't *that* big.

"Here." She unfolded the worn piece of paper she pulled out next and pointed to the drawing of the rainbow-colored ball she'd shown him the other day. "It's just this. I think you know where it is."

"Well, you're wrong about that," said Sully. "I don't even know *what* it is."

"Yes, you do. You just don't know that you know yet."

"Oh-h-h-kay. Why can you see what happened to me when no one else can?"

"You already asked me that."

"Well, you didn't answer."

"It takes one to know one," she said. "Maybe it's just because whatever is inside of you is inside of me, too. But different, I suppose."

"I have no idea what you just said."

"Everyone's jumbled to some degree," she said. "Messed up. Looking for an answer. A solution."

"I'm talking about my face," said Sully. "Can we please stay on that for a minute?"

"Take a look." She dug into her purse again and yanked out a hand mirror this time. The tarnished silver handle was decorated with intricate scrolls and inlay, which wound up and around the shield-shaped mirror. Some fancy letters were etched on the back, too complicated for Sully to decipher.

The Purse Lady pushed the mirror in front of his face and then eased in beside him, so they were both looking at the same image.

"Like I said, messed up. Now that your mouth is right side up, your frown is just a frown."

"I know my face *is* messed up. What I'm asking you is *how* and *why*? How did this happen to me? Please ... you have to help me. It's freaking me out."

"How should I know." She shrugged.

"Well, why can—"

"I see you when no one else can?" she said. "What makes you think you're so invisible?"

Saying this, she shifted the mirror over. The image

looking back at them now was the Purse Lady's own face, but in it her mouth wobbled in the wrinkled hollow of her left cheek, and tragic, red-rimmed eyes balanced along her jawline. Her ears fanned out on either side of her forehead, while her pink nose sniffled sideways on her chin.

Sully's stomach turned over, and his heart felt heavy with bottomless sorrow. Pushing the feeling away, he pulled away from the lady.

"What's going on? Are you the one who did this to me? Are you some kind of witch? I don't believe in witches."

"Don't be so rude."

Sully lunged forward and grabbed the mirror's handle. He looked from the reflective glass to the lady's real face, which looked normal, and back again.

"Takes one to know one," she said again. "Here, help me with this."

She made a movement to shift her stash of items into Sully's arms, but he pushed his hands out in front of him as he walked backward.

"You're freaking me out."

"You were freaked out long before you met me."

"There's something really wrong with you," he said.

"I never said there wasn't."

"Stay away from me."

"Suit yourself." She shoveled the paraphernalia back into her apparently bottomless purse. "You get what you give."

CHAPTER 24

In desperation, even though he felt a little stupid doing it, Sully googled witches and spells about altering people's faces. Surprisingly, there were lots of sites that offered answers. Once inside the various web pages, however, he ended up with the same number of answers he had when he started. Zero.

Besides one site that offered a little chant to give your enemy red eyes, and another that involved candles, water, herbs, and another chant to get rid of acne, most of the others boiled down to the same thing: spells can't really change your appearance, but they can change the way you feel about yourself, which, in turn, can change the way you look. In other words, if you want to be more attractive, you just have to gain greater confidence.

What a crock, Sully thought. He didn't care about looking attractive. He just wanted to look normal. Normal enough that he could glide through Grade 9 without drawing unwanted attention to himself.

Useless preaching about mind over matter was not going to help Sully in his current predicament, and neither, apparently, was the Purse Lady. He wasn't sure what to make of Mr. C., but the old bat with the purse was definitely someone he was going to avoid.

But what about what she showed me in that mirror? He tried to push the thought from his head. She was obviously crazy. Right? But she was also the only one who could really see him. Should he avoid her or should he try again? Sully continued this argument with himself until his head hurt with thinking and he fell asleep.

Sully's first class passed without incident for a change, but before he rounded the corner to English, his stomach twisted as he heard his name spoken in whispers.

Partway down a side hallway near her classroom, Wippet huddled deep in conversation with her wife, Ms. Hamada, who was also the guidance counselor. Dodging an intervention, he crossed the main hallway to approach the class from the other side, but still felt Ms. Hamada's eyes on him in response to a nod in his direction from Wippet.

Almost as if she'd been waiting for him, Blossom appeared at his elbow out of nowhere. She hooked her arm in his and marched him into the classroom.

"Stop that." Sully pulled his arm away and looked around for Dodger.

"Oh, stop being so silly, Bee Boy," she said. "I don't have cooties."

She'd piled more daffodils on her cheekbone, obliterating the smeary purple-green background of yesterday. The red that had outlined her eyes had been replaced with black eyeliner.

"I'm not afraid of cooties," Sully said. "And stop calling me that."

"Just sit," she said. "I've taken the liberty of outlining the essay."

"You're not sick of shadows today?" he said.

"If that was meant as concern, there's no need to worry," she said.

Sully snorted.

"And if it was meant as a jab, you're wasting your time."

"Whatever," he said.

"Well, good then. Moving on. How do you want to divide up the essay?"

"You're the one with all the answers."

"Morsixx is right. You're incredibly ornery."

"Morty called me ornery?"

"His name is Morsixx, and you know that. And he used a different word, but it amounts to the same thing."

"What word?"

"Cantankerous?" she said. "Maybe it was hostile. Either way, it means the same thing. But it's pretty clear what it's covering up."

"I'm not covering anything up," said Sully.

"You're right there," said Blossom. "Your victim syndrome is as plain as the nose on your face."

Sully's hand shot to his nose, still perched on his right cheek.

"What are you saying?" He narrowed his eyes, which was no small feat, given they were lodged in his ears. He looked in Blossom's eyes for any clue that she could see what he really looked like.

"Which word are you having trouble with? Syndrome?"

"What?"

"A syndrome is a—"

"I know what a syndrome is." Sully turned to face the front as Ms. Wippet took her place by the blackboard. "And quit talking," he whispered. "You're going to get me in trouble with Wippet again."

"You are a serious piece of work." Blossom shook her head. "But never you mind. I'm up to the challenge."

Sully shifted his chair away from her and opened his book, pretending to be engrossed.

"If you really want to escape Tank's attention," Blossom leaned closer to Sully, "you should be embracing your friends, not ostracizing them."

Startled by the warmth of Blossom's breath on his neck, Sully whipped his head in the direction of her voice, so they ended up nose-to-nose.

"'Like the herd animals we are,'" she said. "'We sniff warily at the strange one among us'. Loren Eiseley."

"What?"

"Anthropologist. Philosopher. Scientist," she said. "Not afraid to embrace all the strange and disparate parts of himself, Bee Boy. You could learn from him."

"What are you talking about?"

"Here." She slid one of her hands under his and pressed something into his palm.

"Eyes front, Sullivan," said Wippet.

Blossom winked at him as she sat back in her seat.

Sully scrunched his hand over the piece of paper Blossom had deposited and pressed his lips together.

"A thousand pardons, Ms. Wippet." Blossom stood

dramatically and put her palm to her chest. "This is actually my fault. I was just giving him my email address."

Sully reddened as the class hooted and whistled.

"So we can communicate regarding our essay." Blossom enunciated the words slowly and loudly over the crowd. "Honestly, what grade are you people in? In any event, please do continue, Ms. Wippet."

"Why, thank you for your permission, Blossom." Wippet raised her eyebrows. "Quiet down, class. And you ... take your seat."

She directed this last remark at Dodger, who stood by the doorway, smiling at Sully. As Wippet turned her attention back to the lesson, Dodger sauntered back to his seat. He held his phone up to his face and mimed a movie camera in Sully's direction.

CHAPTER 25

Early mornings, coupled with the exertion of walking and the strain of keeping himself under the radar, were taking their toll. By Friday, Sully found himself jolting awake in classes he didn't remember falling asleep in. The weekend promised an oasis of sleep, but it also meant he was only two days away from his Sex Ed presentation.

Never mind that now. Blissful sleep carried him far away from all of it as soon as his head hit the pillow after dinner.

Until he woke with a start, not remembering, for the life of him, where he was.

As his brain slowly pawed its way to full consciousness, a dribble of spit slid down Sully's forehead and under his hairline. He opened his eyes to a deeper darkness, as cold air surfed along his skin and raised goosebumps in places the wind shouldn't have been able to reach.

His right ear seemed to have slipped off his face altogether, snagged in the knots of his long brown curls and straining for any sound that might be a clue. His ankles burned with the pressure of the rope.

The rope?

Fearing the worst, Sully raised his left hand to his face and flexed his fingertips to tease out the numbness. He shouldn't have been able to see anything in the inky blackness, but somehow his palm glowed around the edges, emitting enough light for Sully to see it clearly.

The Black Spot!

Panicking, he arched his back, and then jack-knifed forward in a vain attempt to grab his ankles. Which was ridiculous, really. Even if he'd been able to get hold of the rope, he'd never be able to untie it. And if he did, he'd probably break his back in the fall.

As it was, the movement served only to tighten the snare that pinched painfully, as his naked body swung back and forth and upside down from the limb of the tree.

A flash of light flooded the park. Blinded by the sudden glare, Sully first raised his hands to his face again, and then veered them higher to cover his middle, front and back. The shadowed outlines of spectators revealed themselves, blocking out spaces of light. He'd expected Tank, Ox, and Dodger, but apparently the entire school had been invited. It was like looking out at a crowded movie theater, only everyone was standing across the width of what Sully realized was True Street. The crooked frame of Mr. C., silhouetted against the sky, juggled lightning between his upraised canes.

The crowd showed no emotion at first. Some whispered behind cupped hands, others pointed furtive fingers. Tank stood dead center, but it was Dodger who started things rolling.

"Hey, Sally," he said. "Catch!"

All at once, a series of hard green walnut pods pelted Sully's naked flesh, as the crowd now roared with unconcealed laughter.

"I thought you were a girl, Bella," Winston bent down to look in Sully's face. "But it's like a little sausage."

Sully didn't have enough hands to cover himself up. Blinking away tears, he looked up a second time to find Morsixx standing before him.

"I tried to warn you, Dude. You forgot about your inner Kermit."

"I am half sick of shadows." Blossom peered over Morsixx's shoulder. Tattooed flowers writhed off her face. The vines extended like grasping fingers. They wove themselves into Sully's hair and crept up the sides of his face.

"I am half sick of shadows," she repeated. "But there are no shadows here, Bee Boy. You can see that, right?"

"You're not good at hiding," Winston shook his head. "Not good at all."

The vines slithered around the back of Sully's head, tightening like a noose. As Morsixx and Blossom stepped back into the crowd, the intense pressure released, but something more than the vines seemed to have come undone.

Sully's right ear teased itself loose from his hair and landed sideways in the leaves beneath him. His nose followed and tumbled with a plop amongst a dozen halved walnut pods that themselves looked like little pigs' noses.

His mouth spiraled sideways, and his lips detached with a slight sucking sound. His right eye, still lodged in his left ear canal, cartwheeled off his face and into the growing mound of body parts.

"You weren't looking where you were going," said the Purse Lady, who shuffled into view. "Look what happened to your face."

She stooped down to pick up Sully's eye and held

it up to the light, where it glowed like a little rainbow. Smiling, she popped it into her voluminous black purse.

"Hey!" said Sully's mouth, spitting out leaves. "That belongs to me!"

"I knew you'd help me find it," said the lady.

The top of her purse yawned open, as she laid it on the ground and shoveled the other pieces of Sully's face inside. Shouldering her purse and snapping it shut, she trundled off into the crowd.

The single eye remaining on Sully's face succumbed to gravity. It dropped to the earth in front of him and stared up at his face, which was now entirely devoid of features. A breeze shifted leaves to cover the eye, plunging Sully into darkness again, but not before he saw himself for what he was.

He was nobody.

CHAPTER 26

Sully jolted awake, this time for real. Soaked with sweat, he pawed his face and panted in relief to feel his nose, his mouth, his ear-ensconced eyes. Still in the wrong place, but at least they were there.

Afraid to go back to sleep, he decided to finish the rest of his Sex Ed presentation. While he had the story more or less down, he needed some visuals to go along with it. With remnants of the nightmare nipping at him, he cobbled some images together over the next hour and then slept the rest of the weekend.

But he needed more than sleep to prepare him for Monday morning.

Just be funny, he coached himself as he walked toward class. *And confident*, he thought as he darted a look at Tank. *So it looks like I respect myself.*

I do respect myself. I can do this.

He stood in front of the class as the bell rang. Despite his manufactured bravado, his knees knocked together with such force, they were in danger of dislocating each other. His tongue felt like an old sock, while his nose gyrated in frantic circles.

"What is white and has wings but cannot fly?" he began.

No hands shot up in answer to his riddle, but Sully had expected this. Starting with a joke was a good ploy, though, he thought. It would loosen them up and set the right tone.

He saw he was going to have to work at it a bit, though. Some of his classmates sat with their arms crossed, their heads on a slight angle, their eyes narrowed. His mother often struck that pose when she suspected him of lying. Others lounged back in their chairs, resting their heads against upraised arms. There was a hint of amusement in the eyes of these students, but not the kind that laughs at a lame joke about feminine protection. More like a spider watching an oblivious fly circle in for a landing. Still others made no pretense of paying attention at all. Sully noticed, with relief, that Tank was one of these.

"Okay," said Sully. "We'll come back to that one. What do Moses and Kotex have in common? Anyone?"

A kid in the back row snorted awake, eliciting laughter from the rest.

"We'll come back to that one, too, then," Sully said. "Okay. Well. My topic is menstruation, which should really be called womenstruation, because men don't get it."

Sully's lips had taken on a life of their own. They wavered in opposite directions to push his memorized narrative into a vacuum of silence. And his last joke proved prophetic, because it appeared that none of the guys got it.

"So, you've all heard about Noah's flood, right? Well, it's kind of like that. Only the flood was forty days, and what we're talking about is only twenty-eight. And another difference is that Noah's flood only came once, but what we're talking about comes every month. So, they're kind of the same and kind of different at the same time. And what we're talking about doesn't have all those animals, either, so there's a difference there, too."

This wasn't coming out exactly as Sully had rehearsed it, but it seemed to be getting his classmates' attention. He noticed that most of them had shifted forward in their seats and were watching him intently.

"When Noah's flood is over, he sends out a white

dove to look for dry land," Sully continued. "And that's a clue to the riddle I started with about the white thing with wings. Because what we're talking about also ends with the help of that white winged thing. So, it's kind of like the white-winged dove. But let's get back to Moses."

Sully clicked on his PowerPoint presentation. The first image on the screen was of baby Moses floating on the river in a basket.

"When women get what we're talking about," he said, "they don't have to worry about a little baby like this coming along."

Click.

On screen now was a large chicken egg with the picture of baby Moses pasted in the middle. A big red x was layered on top of both images.

"So, when a woman's egg doesn't get fertilized," Sully said, "what we're talking about ... well, it happens."

"Explain the fertilization part, Rooster," someone shouted from the back.

"Uh," Sully said. "Uh ... that's not part of my presentation."

"More like not part of your life, Brewster," someone quipped.

"So, you're saying girls lay eggs?" someone asked.

"Not exactly," said Sully. "It's more like Blake's Mob allegory. I'll just get to the next part and it should be clearer."

At least, Sully hoped it would be clearer. More and more it was feeling like someone had hijacked his mouth, as the words that came out made less and less sense, even to him.

Sully's next slide was an image of Moses with his arms raised and the sea parting before him. A two-headed arrow was superimposed, pointing at the divided water with a label that said, "The Red Sea (aka Menstruation)." Surrounding Moses was a flock of white birds, their wings spread, diving at the water.

"So, what we're talking about … aka menstruation … is kind of like the tides of a sea. If there's no baby, the tide comes in and then something has to be done about it. That's where the winged things come in."

What in the world was he talking about? How could he ever have convinced himself any of this made any sense at all?

"Hey, TK!" yelled someone from the back of the class. "What if the girl doesn't like white birds and prefers little white sausages instead."

Now the class was laughing openly. A couple of the

guys started flapping their arms in the back of the class, while others made vulgar motions with their fingers.

"All right, all right, Gentlemen," said Green. "Settle down. We're not in kindergarten here."

Slipping on the sweat that dripped from his hairline, Sully's eyes popped out of his ears and rolled around the sides of his head. It felt strange, but it enabled him to stand sideways with one eye on his PowerPoint and one eye on the class.

"This is more than a little obscure, Brewster," said Green. "Are you going to get to the point?"

In answer, Sully pressed the remote again, but instead of his next slide appearing, the computer screen died.

"Brewster?" said Green.

Sully fumbled with the remote, but the computer was unresponsive.

"I've got it, Sir." Dodger vaulted to the front of the classroom and took the remote from Sully's hand.

"Are you even in my class, young man?" Green squinted at Dodger, whose features were mostly hidden under his ball cap, which he had turned to the front.

"Ah, here's the problem." Dodger ignored the question. "Just a disconnected cord, Sir."

The computer sparked to life under Dodger's flying

fingers, and, as he pressed the icon to reopen the presentation, he handed the remote back to Sully.

"She's all yours, Sally."

"Get on with it, Brewster," said Green. "And try to get back on topic."

Flustered, Sully looked at his feet as he pressed the remote, so it was only after the class erupted with laughter that he looked at the screen himself.

Staring back at him was a shot of himself, shoveling handfuls of tampons into his backpack. A caption along the bottom read: *Always carry extra in case of emergency.*

Turning to face the screen, Sully put one hand up to block the image while pressing the off button with his other. Unresponsive to Sully's efforts, the image broke up into little confetti pieces that flew off the screen, only to be replaced by another and then another picture of Sully, tripping down the school stairs with dozens of tampons trailing behind him.

Sully pointed the remote right at the screen and jabbed at the buttons until the screen went black. The laughter cut off abruptly as if it, too, were controled by the remote.

"Very entertaining, Brewster," said Green. "But I fail to

see how any of what you've presented today has answered any of the questions on the assignment sheet."

"But that's not even—" Sully said.

"No excuses, Brewster," said Green. "All of you—"

Hoots and whistles drowned out whatever Green was about to say next.

"Guy ... Pad! Guy ... Pad!" the crowd chanted, many of them resuming the wing flapping and lewd gestures.

When Sully looked back at the screen, another caption spiraled, Star Wars style, out of the screen's black abyss: *guyPad—He's Everywhere!*

A staccato of images followed, illustrating the point: Sully crawling through the parking lot on his hands and knees; Sully in mid flail on the back of the bathroom door; Sully spread-eagled on top of Morsixx.

Sully's eyes chased his ears around the circumference of his face, while his mouth made an apparent effort to turn itself inside out.

Flashes of Green ineffectively waving his arms at the class spiraled in and out of Sully's line of vision, as his eyes rolled around his face like horses on a merry-go-round.

The classroom walls rushed Sully from every side, and the jeers of his classmates sounded far away.

Darkness seeped around the edges of his vision like ink. The last thing he saw before he hit the ground was Tank's impassive but pointed stare from the back of the classroom.

CHAPTER 27

"You're coming with us, Dude."

Sully opened his right eye to a blurry prism of color. The voice in his right ear belonged to Morsixx, but it was the fluid outline of Blossom that leaned over him. A garden of wildflowers accented the warm earth tone of her face. Her multi-colored hair glowed so brightly it made his eye hurt.

How was Blossom here? She wasn't even in this class.

"The herd has gone beyond sniffing, Bee Boy," she whispered, and bent so close that her purple scarf tickled his messed-up face, before she swept it dramatically over her shoulder.

"Some boy in your class texted Morsixx who texted me," Blossom continued. "Come on. You're coming with us."

Sully didn't move. Not only had his ears migrated

to his forehead, they were also on the wrong side of his head, and opposite to his eyes, which had buried themselves upside down in the concave depression of his temples. Deciphering the false cues this delivered him, Sully squinted open his left eye to see Morsixx, his tall, linear, absence of color a relief after Blossom's rainbow riot.

Still, a hammer relentlessly pounded inside Sully's skull. "Go away," he said.

"Not this time, Dude."

"Take him to the school nurse to get looked at." Green's addled expression made it clear Sully was inconvenient roadkill.

"Oh, we'll take care of him all right. Mr. Green, is it?" said Blossom. "And we're going to report you at the same time. What kind of teacher would let this happen in his classroom?"

"Young lady—" Green began.

"Save it, Mr. Green." The flowers on Blossom's face suddenly looked like lethal weapons. Green took an involuntary step back, gawping and floundering as if he'd been slapped.

"Let us help you up," she said to Sully.

"I can take care of myself." Sully's nose wagged uncomfortably on his bottom lip and little spots converged before his eyes as he sat up.

"Right, Dude. You're doing a good job of that."

"I know you're worried about being seen with us," said Blossom. "But even you should realize you've done more damage on your own than we could possibly inflict."

The image of his sabotaged PowerPoint flashed into Sully's head. In his mind's eye, he saw what he hadn't at the time. Tank's eyes had traced his every move, like he was adding up a string of numbers on a calculator.

This vision was followed by another sliver of memory—a parade of faces filing past him, glancing down at his prostrate body as if he were a cadaver at a funeral.

Morsixx took the jump drive from Green and pulled Sully to his feet.

"Damage control," said Blossom. "You need a plan. Let's go."

The trio took the back door out, avoiding the office.

"We're taking the rest of the day off," said Blossom. "This is no time to trust the adults."

"You gotta chill, Dude. You're giving them what they want."

"Oh, and you're not?" said Sully.

"Actually, he's not," said Blossom. "Morsixx's armor is that he doesn't care."

"Yah, well, that's not going to help you when they strip all your stupid Emo armor off you and hang you upside down from a tree," said Sully.

"They're not after me," said Morsixx. "Don't you get it? They're looking for a victim."

"So, those signs they put on our locker were signs of friendship?" Sully said. "Wake up. They've got you pegged as a victim just as much as they've pegged me."

"That could have happened, Dude, but they lost interest."

"You don't know anything," said Sully. "Look, I know you're trying to help, but how do you expect to help me when you can't even help yourself. And you," he said, turning to Blossom. "Easy for you when you can't possibly be chosen."

"What, because I'm a girl?"

"What's with all your stupid tattoos, anyway?" said Sully.

"Stop being so rude," she said. "I know more about this than you'll ever know."

"What, from all your books? You think reading about something's the same thing as living it?"

"I'm not talking about books," she said.

"Look at you. You probably come from some hippy happy family, who all bond and sit around reading together, and painting sunshine and rainbows on each other's faces. Do you get your makeup tips from your mother?"

"That's enough, Dude." Morsixx stopped and towered in front of Sully.

"My mother's dead," said Blossom. The flowers on her face bunched together as if someone was crushing them.

Sully's eyes skulked backward until they were hidden under his hair.

"Oh," he said.

"You beaten us up enough so we can talk now?" said Morsixx.

"I'm ... you know, sorry," Sully said to Blossom.

"Forget it," said Blossom. Her scarf billowed like purple wings behind her as she ran ahead. She veered to the right, off the path, before suddenly disappearing.

"Wait up," said Morsixx.

"Where'd she go?" said Sully.

Up ahead, the walking path pulled away from the train tracks, meandering left to follow the narrow river that snuck under the rails. Tall grasses and bramble hid the steep banks, as the river raced to feed the lake in the heart of the park, before spilling precipitously over a sharp fall at Main Street and bolting under the road for the next town.

"Down here!" Blossom called back. "Come on. It's beautiful!"

Morsixx strode in the direction of Blossom's voice. He pushed through the weeds and disappeared himself. Sully followed at a slower pace, turning his head to the side, so at least one of his eyes had a chance of making out the path Morsixx and Blossom had taken.

Despite his wariness, Sully's feet slipped out beneath him, and he found himself sliding the rest of the way on his butt, down the sharp incline of the riverbank.

"Grab those stalks on your way down to slow your—" said Morsixx.

With his arms thrown in front to stave off the various weeds that whipped his face, Sully slid past Morsixx and Blossom, before landing in mud and goose droppings at the water's edge.

"Thanks for the warning," Sully said, as he looked up at them.

"Look around." Blossom snapped photos with her phone. "It's like something out of a poem! Smile, Bee Boy!"

Morsixx and Blossom leaned against the large concrete pad that anchored the tracks halfway up the riverbank. Gripping the ledge, they pulled themselves up into the small alcove under the rails, and then pivoted to face the steel trusses under the rail bridge. The view yawned over crisscrossed steel beams, open to the water underneath, but banked on either side by rusted walls decorated with graffiti.

"Come up here!" said Blossom.

"Why?" said Sully. "I'm all wet. It looks like I peed myself. Thanks a lot."

"Oh, quit your whining and get up here," she said.

Sully grabbed the stalks he'd missed on the way down and struggled up the incline. Failing his first few attempts, he took Morsixx's offered hand, but scraped his stomach on the way up into the alcove under the bridge.

"Nice," he said, lifting his shirt. "See this? I'm bleeding. Are you trying to help me or kill me?"

"Like she said, Dude. Your whining is getting old."

"So, Bee Boy, let's take this from the beginning."

"My name's not Bee Boy! My name is Sully! Sullivan Brewster! Why can nobody get that?"

"Calm down," said Blossom. "Bee Boy is a term of affection. There's no need to get hysterical."

"I'm not hysterical. But we're probably only talking weeks now. By this time at the end of the month ... by the end of October ... Tank will definitely have chosen his victim, just like the last two years. And it's not going to be me. Period, end of story."

"Then you have to stop shooting yourself in the foot," said Blossom. "Honestly, the way you're going about this, it's almost like you're asking to be targeted."

"She's right, Dude. The more you try to hide, the more they see you."

Sully sat between them, one eye on each.

"I'm just trying to fly under the radar," he said. "Just till this is over."

"Under the radar, huh?" said Blossom. "Maybe I should call you Bat Boy, then, because if you keep this up, you're going to have more than radar in common with a bat. Like hanging upside down from a tree for—"

"Okay, okay." Sully let out a breath it felt like he'd been holding for months. "You're right. You're both right. Geez, how did it all get so bad? I made an idiot of myself with my stupid presentation, and it wasn't just Dodger's photos."

"From what I've heard, I'm not going to·argue with you, Dude."

"I was just trying to get through it without embarrassing myself, but even I couldn't understand what I was saying."

"What photos?" asked Blossom.

"You *see*!" said Sully. "It's not all my fault. Tank, Dodger, Ox ... they've obviously been stalking me from the beginning. They made it look like I horde tampons. Like I love tampons. They showed photos of me hanging in the boys' bathroom with a wedgie; and then when I fall from the door on top of Morsixx, they took a picture of that, too. Worse than that, they staged it. They're out to get me!"

"Okay, Dude, slow down. Let's figure out where it all started and maybe we can go backward from there."

"It started on day one, Morsixx, the very first day. When I get into Sex Ed late on the first day, Green goes on and on, thinking I'm a girl. And you don't help in English, Blossom. Don't you know Dodger's in that class? It was you that caused Wippet to have me read that ridiculous poem in front of the class; and then you got us in trouble by passing notes. If you really want to help me, stop trying to help me."

"Don't try to pin that on me," said Blossom. "Try paying attention for once. Do your homework. If you want to backpedal out of this, it's going to take a little effort."

"Stick with us, Dude. Stop blaming everyone else and stop trying to go it alone."

"And stop being so afraid," said Blossom. "Don't you know that bullies can smell fear? It fuels them. You think it would make them stop, but it doesn't. It makes them worse."

She picked up a loose chunk of concrete as she said this and threw it at the steel trusses. Sully jumped as it hit one of the walls with such force that it ricocheted off several beams, before clunking in the water below.

"Nice arm," said Morsixx, but even in the dim light, Sully noticed the pinched look of the flowers on Blossom's face.

"Thanks," she said, as the flowers gradually unpinched. "Anyway. What we're trying to say is that there's strength in numbers."

True, thought Sully to himself. Plus, maybe the opposite of what he'd previously thought was true. Maybe the best way to become invisible was to actually hang out with the two of them. Between the extremes of their ridiculousness—Morsixx's all-black wardrobe, his new name and laidback ways; Blossom's tattoos, bright colors and encyclopedic verbosity—who would even notice him? And then he hated himself for even thinking this.

"Stick with us, Dude. Everyone needs friends. Okay?"

"Okay," said Sully. "Thanks."

It would be good to have them watching out for him, he thought. It had been hard going it alone and, for all their strangeness, they were the closest to friends that he had. At least they wouldn't intentionally hurt him.

CHAPTER 28

Even before Tuesday started, Sully could feel that things were turning around. Because he was no longer avoiding Blossom and Morsixx, and was thus able to take the bus, the extra hour of sleep alone vastly improved his mood. No more fear of running into the Purse Lady, and no more long, early morning walks.

His stepdad had an early meeting, and his mom and Eva left before breakfast for a school field trip, which freed Sully to have a nice, slow breakfast in daylight. Fulfilling their promise, Morsixx and Blossom kept him out of harm's way on the bus.

It was a relief not to have to carry his backpack around with him everywhere, since he resumed using his shared locker with Morsixx, and he found it surprisingly calming to have a normal conversation with Morsixx before class. Mr. Green was actually courteous to Sully after Blossom, true to her word, had reported Monday's incident to the office; and Wippet gave them the class to work on their essays. Winston didn't try to hug him or play hide and seek. At lunch, Sully took a seat in the cafeteria with Morsixx and Blossom, just like a normal kid, with no one looking at him or laughing at him.

It was his best day of high school so far, and he began to think his paranoia really had got the best of him.

Until a table erupted in laughter by the window.

"Hey, Brewster!" someone shouted. "Nice confession!"

A guy down the table held up his phone and pressed the play button, revealing a video loop of Sully falling down the riverbank over and over. When the kid turned up the sound, a voice broadcast across the cafeteria. The syntax and intonation were off—sound bytes clearly edited and reordered—but the voice was definitely Sully's:

"My name is Sully. Sullivan Brewster. I'm a girl. When I fall for boys, I make out like some sex pervert. How did it all get so bad? When it's my time of the month ... when I get my period with no warning, it looks like I peed myself. Geez, I'm bleeding. Why can nobody get that? That's why I love tampons. If you want to help me, just buy me tampons. Thanks a lot."

Every eye in the cafeteria veered from the screen to Sully himself, who sat, mid-chew, his eyes riveted to the screen, which started to play the video again.

There were only two people with him at the rail bridge where this video was shot, and they were sitting right beside him.

CHAPTER 29

Sully's eyes wobbled uncertainly toward each other. They crossed in an arc over his mouth and crawled into the hollows of his cheeks. They blinked in slow motion, one at Blossom and the other at Morsixx, taking note of the protest, defense, outrage, and challenge that charged across their faces.

Their mouths were forming words, but Sully's ears had folded over each other, effectively blocking out sound. The entire scene played out like a silent movie at quarter speed, giving Sully's eyes ample time to gulp in every detail of the activity around him.

How could he have been so stupid? Blossom had pretended she was taking pictures because the rail bridge was like a poem, when she really must have been capturing him on film. Morsixx had pulled him up, not to help him, but so that he'd be closer to the microphone. He had wanted so badly to believe they were really trying to help him, and part of him still couldn't believe they'd done this to him. But it was the only explanation, because they were the only ones who'd been there.

He pushed himself away from the table, noticing out of the corner of his eyes that his chair fell soundlessly in slow motion. Pockets of students rose to their feet, crowding around screens and throwing their heads back, grins cracking their faces with gaping black holes. Fists pumped the air. Bodies swayed. Hands clapped. Only when he reached the door to the atrium did the roar of laughter crash around him all at once. As Morsixx grabbed him by the shoulders, and Blossom stepped in front of him, their voices caught up with the movement of their mouths as if part of a movie that had just stopped buffering.

"... exactly what we're talking about!" Blossom's hands were on her hips, as if she'd been scolding him.

"Stop, Dude. We've got your back."

Sully yanked away from Morsixx and maneuvered to the side.

"That's what you call having my back?"

"I know it seems bad, Dude, but—"

"How could you do this to me?"

"How could *we* do this to you? Don't be an idiot," said Blossom.

"No one else was there!"

"That we were aware of," said Blossom.

"You can't seriously believe we'd do that," said Morsixx.

"It doesn't matter what I believe. It happened. Which is proof you can't help me."

"You think going it alone is going to make you less vulnerable, Dude?"

But Sully wasn't listening. He clamped his hands over his ears, which were in the process of receding under his hairline, and charged out of the school.

"Bella!"

"Leave me alone," Sully said.

"I saw your movie, Bella. You're famous!"

"Even you can't be that stupid." Sully pushed past Winston.

Unbalanced by Sully's nudge, Winston fell to one knee, causing him to drop his books and scrape his palms.

"Bella?" Winston's wide eyes, shiny and full, shifted alternately between Sully and the blood on his hands.

"Stop your crying and grow up," Sully said as he walked backward away from him.

"Are you okay, Bella?" Winston's bottom lip trembled.

"What do you think, Winston? Do I look okay to you? Oh, yah. You don't have a clue, do you? You think everything's a stupid game, because everyone tiptoes around you and tries to make you feel safe and happy. Well, I've got news for you. Everyone's lying to you. Nothing is okay. The real world is rotten and mean, and all people want to do is hurt you. The sooner you figure that out the better."

"That's not what I think, Bella."

"Your problem is you don't think at all, Winston. And my stupid name isn't Bella, okay? Just leave me alone."

By the time the park deposited him onto True Street, Sully paused, doubled over from a stitch in his side. As he leaned for a moment on Mr. C's fence, Pumbaa fell on the sidewalk in front of him.

"So, what's that supposed to mean, Mr. C.!" he shouted at the house. For emphasis, he ground the little plastic Pumbaa into the sidewalk, much as he'd done emotionally to Winston just minutes before. A few feet away, he saw Charlie Brown half-buried in the dirt, upside down.

"Well, that's great." He grabbed the fence and shook it. "That's just great! What are you trying to tell me that I don't already know! I'm a loser! I get it!"

The Sleeping Beauty character toppled as a result of Sully's tantrum, but the twist tie attaching her to the knight kept her from plummeting to the sidewalk. Darth Vader, Goyle, and The Riddler, unaffected by Sully's little tantrum, held firm.

Placing his hands on the fence a third time, Sully became aware that the curtains of the front window had parted, and that Mr. C. was staring at him, shaking his head.

"You don't know anything!" Sully shouted. "You're just a stupid, senile old man who plays with dolls!"

Pulling back from the fence, Sully kicked Charlie Brown before lighting off for Perdu and sprinting the rest of the way home.

CHAPTER 30

"Stop playing with your food, Sullivan. Come on, eat up. I made brownies for dessert."

Tick, thought Sully. Mom noticed my picking.

"It's really good, Mom," Sully said. "I don't know. My stomach's just feeling a bit woozy."

"Did you skip lunch?"

You could say that, Sully mused.

"You're probably just over-hungry. Eat up and you'll feel better."

"No, it's not that. The thing is, I'm not hungry. Or at least, I am, but I'm just not feeling well."

"You have to eat your dinner before you can have dessert," said Eva. "Brownies, Rooster. Your favorite."

"You can have my share of brownies, Eva," Sully said. "Mom, I think I need to lie down for a bit. Can I be excused?"

"How about I keep your plate warm." Mom eyed him with concern. "I'll check in on you in an hour?"

"No." Sully injected just the right amount of whine and breathlessness. He'd decided that the best way to be invisible at Wild Forest was to disappear completely. He intended to milk his fabricated illness for as long as he could, and the best time to launch an operation of this sort was dinner the evening before.

"No," he said again. "I think I just need to get to bed early. I'm sure I'll feel better in the morning."

This last part, he knew, was genius. Of course, the plan was to get steadily worse throughout the night. With the bathroom beside his parents' room, he'd set his alarm to do some impressive retching in the middle of the night.

The cafeteria video had decided things for him. One way or another, he'd find a way to be invisible, and step one was to stay away from school as much as possible. Thinking about it, he knew Morsixx and Blossom weren't responsible. More than that, he knew they really did care about him. But that didn't mean they could save him, and the video was proof of that.

"Oh," said Eva. "I almost forgot! Jennifer's brother, Nathan, said you were in a movie at school today, Rooster."

"A movie?" said Mom.

"Nathan said the whole school watched it," said Eva. "You're famous, Rooster!"

"Nathan must be talking about my PowerPoint presentation for Mr. Green," said Sully, thinking fast. "I had to do mine on menstruation."

"Oooh, Vanny," said his stepdad. "Menstruation. That was unlucky."

Mom gave Bill a dirty look.

"What's men station?" asked Eva.

"Just something to do with trains," said Sully, thinking quickly again. "You, know. Train stations, Eva?"

"Oh," Eva said, echoing Bill. "That was unlucky."

You don't know the half of it, thought Sully.

"Why was that unlucky, Dad?" Eva looked confused.

"Did I say unlucky?" said Bill. "I meant lucky! Trains are cool, right, Sully?"

"Sure," said Sully. "Trains are cool. But it wasn't the whole school who saw it." *Yah, it was*, he thought. "Just my health class."

"Are you sure you can't eat, Sullivan?" said Mom.

"Maybe in a bit," said Sully. "I'm pretty sure if I just lie down and get some rest, I'll feel better."

Everything was going according to plan. Mom excused Sully from the table and he retreated to his room with his door closed. He was just about asleep, in fact, when the vibration of his phone woke him.

Morsixx. After the fifth call, Sully turned his phone off. He curled up in his blankets with his alarm set for 1 AM.

The clanking of dishes, the polite trill of the phone, the buzz of faraway conversation. All the sounds began to run together in Sully's head, when Mom's voice called from the bottom of the stairs.

"Sullivan?"

CHAPTER 31

"Sullivan, I'm coming in. We need to talk."

Sully pulled the blankets away from his eyes. His mother leaned against the doorframe with the phone in her hand.

"You've not been truthful with me."

A thousand possibilities chased through Sully's brain. Mr. C's fence? Winston's bloody hands? The cafeteria video?

Winston's bloody hands. For the first time since the incident, Sully felt a sting of shame.

"I just got off the phone with your principal," Mom supplied. "She told me you've cut classes two days in a row. She also mentioned your involvement in some incidents she thinks we should talk about. What's this about, Sullivan? Talk to me."

For half a second, Sully contemplated telling his

mom the whole story, but he bit his tongue. Which was above his nose, just under his brow bone. He was beginning to admit to himself that he might just be his own worst enemy, and that his extreme attempts to evade attention were the very things that got him singled out.

Well, all the more reason he needed to make smarter decisions. He knew his mom meant well, but that didn't mean she could save him, any more than Morsixx and Blossom could.

What was it Tank said on that very first bus ride? That he needed to respect himself? Well, part of respecting himself meant trusting his instincts and, right now, his gut told him that letting his mom fight his battles for him was not going to make him seem like less of a loser to Tank.

No. He needed to save himself, and sometimes saving yourself meant not joining the fight. Even whole armies retreat sometimes, when they know the odds are stacked against them.

"Sullivan?"

"Don't worry, Mom. It's true I cut some classes yesterday and today, but it's only because I wasn't feeling well, and I didn't want to worry you."

He held his breath to see if she'd buy it.

"You think this makes me less worried?"

"Really, Mom. I was just trying to make adult decisions for myself."

Ooh, he thought, *that's good.*

Or maybe not. Mom looked dubious at best.

"Look, Sullivan, I don't know what's going on, but that doesn't explain the rest of what Miss Winters said about, quote, incidents. What is she referring to? How can I help you if you withhold information from me?"

"It's not how it looks," said Sully. "I'm starting to feel better now that I've rested a bit. I'll go in early and explain things to Miss Winters, okay?"

Real early, he thought. He'd spend the night forging a sick note from his mom, and slip it in the school office before any of the other students showed up.

"Well, we actually don't have a choice about that," said Mom. "You and I have a meeting with Miss Winters at eight o'clock tomorrow morning."

CHAPTER 32

As Sully and his mother stood outside the principal's office the next morning, Sully's eyes maneuvered in calculated angles across his face like a pair of spies entering an unsecured location.

"Your son is off to a dubious start," Miss Winters began, before Sully and his mother had even taken their seats. "The facts are that your son has been cutting classes and was involved in two incidents involving inappropriate displays of feminine protection."

"Sullivan was *assigned* a presentation on menstruation," said Mom. "He was *required* to speak on the subject."

"Every student in Mr. Green's class was assigned a similar presentation, and none of them caused a school-wide commotion. Nor are any of them truant. When your son does attend class—"

"He has a name," said Mom.

"Of course," said Miss Winters. "But hardly the point. The point is that his teachers inform me that when he deigns to attend class, he is inattentive and unprepared. I've noticed myself that he alienates and is somewhat rude to his fellow students. In my experience," Winters continued, "this kind of behavior often stems from the home. Is there something you want to share with me?"

"Share with you?" said Mom.

"Yes," said Miss Winters. "I see from the file that Sullivan's father has not been part of his life since Sullivan was just a baby. Single parenthood can't be easy."

"Ours is not a single parent household," said Mom. "But even if it was, the point is irrelevant."

Sully turned to look at his mom. It struck him that the quiet measure of her voice was laced with something more dangerous.

"There is nothing wrong with Sullivan's home life," said Mom, "and if I'm not mistaken, we're here to talk about his behavior in *school*."

"The point I'm trying to make, Miss Davidson—"

"*Mrs.* Davidson," said Mom.

"*Mrs.* Davidson." Miss Winters parroted Mom's inflection. Her mouth was smiling but her eyes were not. "The point I'm trying to make ... *Mrs.* Davidson, is that a child's situation at home impacts his behavior at school. The two are inextricably linked."

Sully's mom seemed to be following this conversation, even though Sully himself was becoming increasingly confused.

"Do you have children, Miss Winters?"

"Five hundred and thirty-four of them this year alone, Mrs. Davidson. And I've been an administrator for twenty-seven years, so—"

"I asked you if you had children," said Mom. "Your *own* children."

"Well, no, I—"

"Which qualifies you, exactly how, to pass judgment on parenting?" said Mom. The level of Mom's voice was steadily escalating.

"It qualifies me eminently," said Miss Winters. "With my judgment unclouded by emotional attachments, I'm able to bring decisive objectivity to the upbringing and discipline of the young people who populate the various institutions I've led for the past twenty-seven years."

"Is that so?" said Mom. "Well, I have news for you, Miss Winters. You know about as much about raising a child as I do about astrophysics, which, in case you miss the point, is zilch."

"Mrs. Davidson!" Miss Winters stood so that her spindly frame towered over Sully and his mom.

"There's absolutely nothing wrong with Sullivan's home life."

Sully's mom stood to emphasize the point. She faced Miss Winters eyeball-to-eyeball.

"I have a loving husband who would do anything for our children and, as Sullivan's mother, I would claw and defend Sullivan to the death, if it came to it. If Sully's having troubles I haven't been aware of, thank you for informing me, but casting blame helps no one. Sullivan is an intelligent, sensitive soul, who just needs a couple of years to grow into his own sense of self, which, incidentally, is no different from the other five hundred and thirty-three young people you so superciliously claim as your own."

Mom and Miss Winters stood like mirror opposites across the desk, palms flat, spread fingers extending from rigid arms, brows creased, eyes narrowed.

Sully found himself impressed by how his mother stood up to Winters. And how she stuck up for him—like the proverbial lioness protecting her young. It crossed his mind that even Tank wouldn't be a match for his mother. Nevertheless, he wasn't sure this exchange was really going to do him any favors with Miss Winters in the long run.

"Sullivan." His mom broke stance first. "You won't cut any more classes, is that clear?"

Sully nodded.

"And you and I will talk about everything at dinner this evening, understand?"

Sully nodded again. His lips zigzagged down his face to rest on the left side of his jaw, while his ears circled in unison around the circumference of his face. And that wasn't all. His brain was also doing some pretty impressive gymnastics, as it flipped between relief at having his mom fight his battles and fear that he'd be pegged as a momma's boy.

"Good, then," said Mom. "I think we're done here. Grab your backpack and get to class, Sullivan."

As they exited the office, Sully spotted Tank in the hallway.

"I'm not feeling very well," said Sully. And he really wasn't. His eyes spun in their sockets and his stomach felt like a ship in the middle of a perfect storm. He might as well take advantage of Mom's lioness instincts.

"I agree that was unpleasant," said Mom, "but I'm sure what you're feeling is just nerves, and this wouldn't be the best time for you to miss classes, don't you think? Plus, I'm pretty sure there's more to this than you're telling me, so you and I do need to talk this evening. Okay, Sullivan?"

"Okay, Mom." He realized the only way out of this was to play along. "See you after school."

He maneuvered to the other side of his mother to evade Tank's notice. Nerves or not, his stomach really didn't feel good. Once he was sure Mom was gone, he bolted for the bathroom.

It was a good call. Surveying his breakfast, now floating in the toilet bowl, he doublechecked that no pieces of his face had dislodged in the process. Satisfied, he flushed twice and staggered to the sink to splash water on his face.

Okay, he thought. *I can handle this. I must have some of Mom's genes.* And in that moment, he really did feel better.

He turned off the tap and looked in the mirror. What he saw was far worse than anything he'd seen since this whole nightmare began. But it wasn't his distorted facial features that caught his attention this time, even though they were currently putting on quite a show.

Scrawled in black marker across the mirror was a list

of three names. Numbers two and three were kids he'd never heard of, but at the top of the list was a single name: "Sally."

Sully was on the short list.

CHAPTER 33

The short list.

One of the students on this list would receive the Black Spot in the next seven days, and, within thirteen days after that, would be fully exposed in the Naked Niner attack.

That was the pattern, and part of the torture was knowing that it was imminent but not knowing exactly when. You could protect yourself if you knew when. You could surround yourself with allies. But without a firm date, part of the way they got you was with the anxiety you dressed yourself in each morning.

Sully tore out of the bathroom. He staggered drunkenly under the weight of his backpack until he reached the top of the stairway. As if surfacing after too long under water, he gasped for air and pulled at the tight knots in his neck. His face was like an electronic switchboard on overload, every one of his features pinging, sliding, blinking, colliding in constant motion, and completely out of his control.

Tripping down the stairway, he barged into the school office.

"Miss Winters!"

"You are supposed to be in class, Mr. Brewster."

"They're out to get me! I need your help!"

"Calm down, Mr. Brewster. Who is 'they?'"

"I looked in the mirror. I'm on the short list." He had a sense that hysteria was making him incoherent.

"I'm certain you haven't finished growing. And I hardly think your height is anything to get hysterical about."

"No!" said Sully. "Not the short list. The *short* list."

"You are not making sense and I have a call I need to return." She looked around then, as if afraid Sully's mother might be within earshot. "Do yourself a favor and blend in, Mr. Brewster. Stop calling attention to yourself. Now get to class."

"But it's in the bathroom, if you'll just follow me," Sully tried again.

"If I'm not mistaken, Mr. Brewster, you and your mother just finished telling me that you're perfectly okay. I'm sure you'll find a way to deal with whatever it is you're talking about, given that you are, as your mother put it, intelligent and sensitive. Perhaps you're just being overly sensitive about your height, Mr. Brewster, and the best cure for that, in my experience, is to face your adversity head on. Embrace who you are and don't concern yourself with others' opinions."

"But you don't understand—"

"Look, Mr. Brewster. I already set aside time for you this morning. By all means, book another meeting with me through the school secretary, but right now, I have other business to attend to and you are supposed to be in class."

Sully nodded and stumbled into the hallway. While his brain fully intended to head to Green's class, his feet carried him out of the school and into the parking lot. His brain and his feet continued to ignore each other until he stepped onto True Street.

Seconds before his head hit the ground, he became aware that something small, round, and green was accelerating toward him at an alarming pace.

CHAPTER 34

"What the—!"

Sully touched his forehead, where something had just whistled past, narrowly missing him. In a defensive reflex, he threw himself on the ground, which caused his eyes to slide sideways. In a chain reaction, his mouth cowered beside his nose and his ears crowded his left jaw.

"Can't you see what's going on?"

Sully turned his head to see Mr. C. hollering and hobbling toward him at breakneck speed. His canes flashed in the sunlight as he darted nimbly round the fence.

"That nearly hit me!" Sully sprang to his feet and thrust his palms before him like stop signs. "What are you, crazy? You could have killed me!"

"If I'd wanted it to hit you, it would have hit you. You are such a nutcase; a nut is what you deserve."

"Stay away." Sully backed away. "I'll call the cops."

"You will not do even that," said Mr. C. He waved one of his canes at the fence. "It seems you will do nothing except run."

As Sully jogged backward, his sleeve snagged on the knight and Sleeping Beauty. The sudden motion spun him around. He landed with his jaw on the rail, eyeball-to-eyeball with Darth Vader. The Madonna figurine's blue cloak and large black backpack were a blur in the background.

"Stupid! Stupid!" Sully pulled his sleeve free and spun in the other direction to make his escape to Perdu.

"Can't you see what's happening?" Mr. C. yelled after him. "Those two are trying so hard to help you. Do you really think it's coincidence that you landed face-to-face with the Vader? Oh-h-h, I'm not supposed to be telling you these things! Perhaps you cannot be helped."

"At least I'm not crazy!" Sully yelled over his shoulder.

"I think maybe you are wrong about that," Mr. C. called after him. "Look at the fence, Boy, just look at it. It's like watching a car crash in slow motion."

As Sully rounded the corner, he whipped his head to the side so his eyes could see where he was going. The Purse Lady jumped into his line of vision.

"My goodness." She shook her head. "Look at you. Are you even trying?"

"No!" Sully pushed past her. "Don't talk to me!"

He ran the rest of the way home and sat at the kitchen table. *The short list*, he thought. *What am I going to do?* He'd pretty well burned his bridges with Miss Winters. He doubted even he'd believe himself after his track record at school to date.

Morsixx and Blossom were willing, but the cafeteria episode proved them incapable.

What about Mom? The thought had passed through his head this morning when they'd met with Miss Winters that Mom might well be a good match for Tank. Out of desperation, he punched Mom's work number into the phone.

"Hello?" The tone of her first word was already making him second-guess himself, but he pushed on.

"Mom," he said. "There's this list at school and I'm on it."

Mom hesitated a beat. "A class list? Does this have to do with that presentation you gave, or the incidents your principal referenced?"

"Well, sort of. I mean, it can't have helped. I mean, I was kind of set up, and—"

"Set up?" said Mom. "By whom?"

"The ones who put me on the list."

"What list are we talking about, Sullivan. And can we talk about this tonight?"

Now that he was actually, on the phone with his mom, Sully remembered why he hadn't gone to her in the first place. Having his mom fight his battles for him would make him more of a target, not less of one. A virtual straight line to the black spot.

"Well," he hedged, "it's not a long list."

He needed to detour this conversation and fast. All he really needed was Mom's permission to stay home so he could evade all of this. If he wasn't at school to receive the Black Spot, they'd have to pick one of the other two.

"So, it's a short list?" said Mom.

"Ahhh," said Sully. "Don't say that."

"Don't say what?" said Mom. "Sullivan, I'm more than a little confused."

That makes two of us, thought Sully.

"Are you on a list or not," said Mom, "and what does it mean if you are? And, more to the point, since I can see that you're calling from home, what does that have to do with you cutting class again?"

"Forget the list, Mom. The truth is, I'm really just not feeling well."

And this certainly was the truth. His heart was racing far too fast, and it felt like someone had a grip on his windpipe.

"Look, Sullivan. You got me out of a meeting. As I said to you this morning, I think what you're feeling is just nerves. Get yourself back to class and we'll talk about all of this after school, okay? Promise me?"

"Okay, Mom," said Sully.

"Bill's working from home today, after he gets back from taking Eva to school, so he can drive you."

A day home hiding from Bill was not going to make things better.

"It's okay, Mom. I think the walk will do me good."

"All right, Sullivan. You understand attending class is important, right? Especially after our meeting this morning?"

"I do," said Sully. "I plan to stay out of trouble."

And that's exactly what he intended to do. Without home to hide out in, he'd find a way to pass the time until school let out and he could legitimately head back home.

To avoid Mr. C and The Purse Lady, he navigated alternate sidewalks with no clear plan of where he was going. Still, even with his cap pulled forward, his hands jammed under his armpits, and his shoulders hunched, he felt as exposed as a worm after a rainstorm.

More by accident than design, he found himself at the foot of the falls. These weren't Angel Falls, or even Niagara, but under the cold, gray October sky, they were unfriendly and menacing. A homeless man had fallen over the edge here when Sully was younger. While the vertical drop wasn't that high, the riverbed was shallow at the base, with numerous jagged rocks. It wasn't the fall that had killed him, it was the landing.

Sully hurried along the walkway into the park, to where the path forked around the lake. Heading right would launch him over the footbridge toward the playground and True Street. Continuing straight would put him on the path he normally took to school. He had no intention of going either place, but off the path ahead was a shallow forest he could hide in.

Scanning for the right place to enter, he realized he was at the entrance to the path that wound under the rail bridge. His first instinct was to point himself in the exact opposite direction. He knew what PTSD was, and this place was a big-time trigger. Just looking at the path caused his chest to tighten and his head to ache.

A crazy mix of emotions flickered through him. Hanging out here with Blossom and Morsixx had made him feel part of something bigger than himself. Like he actually might be able to have good friends, even if they were both a little odd.

But that golden moment had been warped into something monstrous. By opening himself to something good, he'd exposed himself to the worst experience of his life.

And now he was on the short list.

If he was honest with himself, he knew he had already been flagged as a candidate for the Naked Niner, probably from that first day on the bus when he'd literally fallen in Tank's lap. But the video couldn't have helped. It probably sealed the deal. Gift-wrapped him.

But even as he thought this, he realized he had it backward. Dodger must have followed them here. Who else? It wouldn't be hard to hide in all the overgrowth.

But so what? Even if that's the way it happened, it still happened. He couldn't afford to trust anyone again. It was like what Mr. Escrow had asked them to copy off the board last week—a quote from President Obama: "Change will not come if we wait for some other person or some other time. We are the ones we've been waiting for. We are the change that we seek."

Mr. Escrow had explained that these words called upon citizens to stand up for what's right and challenge what's wrong, rather than waiting for someone else to come to the rescue, but Sully decided to put his own spin on it. He decided to go back to his solo mission; to look only to himself for a change in his situation. Or, more correctly, evasion of his situation.

He climbed up, past the graffitied alcove under the tracks and through the tall grass, until he was on the same level as the tracks themselves. It felt private in here. A few feet of sloped gravel left space to sit on either side of the rails, but the overgrowth beyond that on either side enclosed him like the walls of a room.

He sat a few feet from where a train would pass on its way to cross the small river. In front of him, the rails converged to a single point across the water and down the line.

The chill wind bit into his fingers, but it would only be for a little while, and then he could head home. No one would think to look for him here.

But then someone did.

"My name is Sullivan Brewster. I peed myself! Don't look at me! Oooooh!"

CHAPTER 35

Sully jumped to his feet and gawked around like a bobblehead doll, as he tried to locate where the voice was coming from.

"Boo, Sally!"

Dodger leapt out of the bushes and landed within three feet of Sully, who clambered backward to the shallow gravel embankment on the other side of the tracks.

"Not so fast, guyPad." Ox popped out of the bushes on this side, menacing Sully back to the tracks at the center.

"Well, well, well, Sally." Sully turned slowly to see Tank enter the clearing behind Dodger.

"You'd be surprised at how good the acoustics are here, Sally." Dodger held his phone at arm's length, pointed at Sully. "We plan on getting lots of raw footage for another fabulous feature movie. Ready or not, three-two-one ... action!"

Sully scanned the area, looking for a way to escape.

With Tank and Dodger on one side of the tracks and Ox on the other, Sully's only choices were to inch backward along the rails behind him, or forward toward the rail bridge that crossed the small river.

Back seemed the smarter choice, but as he took a step in that direction, Tank sauntered to the middle of the tracks to block Sully's path.

Pivoting in response, Sully tripped and landed on his butt between two ties.

"Riddle me this," said Dodger. "What's physically short, short on self-respect, and is now on a list that is short?"

"Short is not the least of what you are." Tank took a step toward Sully, who jumped to his feet. "It may, in fact, be the best of what you are."

Sully's eyes swooped from one side to the other, as if searching for a way to escape his face. The only open space was now behind him. Over the rail bridge across the river.

"If you had any spine at all, maybe you wouldn't be quite so short." Tank had halved the space between them. All he had to do was reach out his hand and Sully was toast.

"The only thing that might save you is that you're so

pathetic, it's almost boring. It *was* a point of debate, Sally. You're such a loser, there's almost no sport in it."

"Note he said 'almost,'" said Ox, who advanced from Sully's right.

"More!" Dodger filmed with his camera and directed Sully with his free hand. "Give me more! I'm not feeling it, Sally!"

Sully stepped backward. His right foot hesitantly claimed the last rail tie on solid ground before the tracks sprinted over the water ten feet below. The riverbanks were unforgiving here. If Sully jumped to either side, he'd land badly and probably break his neck.

"You don't *have* more, do you, Sally. You don't have nothing. Because that's all you are ... nothing."

Sully took another step back. His eyes plunged under his chin and stared at the foot and a half of almost empty air between the tie under his left foot and the one behind him.

"If I didn't know better," said Tank, "I'd say you were *trying* to get chosen."

Sully's right leg shook as he swung it back to feel for the next tie. He shifted his weight onto it and bent his knees for support. The water was now entirely underneath him. He was committed.

"You don't have the guts to keep going, Sally." Tank steadily closed the space between them. "You're not even good at running away."

Sully jutted his chin up and to the side. He calculated that it was only ten, maybe twelve, feet across the rail bridge to the other side of the river.

"You're asking yourself 'why me?', aren't you, Sally."

That's only ten or twelve steps, Sully reasoned. Surely he could take ten or twelve steps to save himself.

But Sully's left foot seemed to be glued to the tie in front.

"It's because you're weak, Sally." Tank took another step toward him. "And as my dear old dad would say, the weak grow up invisible and useless. Exposing you would actually be doing you a favor."

With his arms out to the side for balance, Sully lifted the enormous weight of his left leg and pulled it back. He toed the air, at first missing and then finding the tie that would move him another step away from Tank.

"You don't even try to stick up for yourself. Invisible doesn't mean safe, Sally. Invisible means dead."

Tank took another step forward. "Let's see what you got, Sally."

Instinct took over, and Sully's feet and brain once

more disconnected. With the prowess of a tightrope walker, he edged steadily backward, bending the knee of the leg in front, pushing it back, finding the rail with the tip of his sneakers, pressing back until his foot hugged the tie. When he realized Tank was no longer following him, his brain caught up, telling him he'd made it halfway to the other side.

Sully's eyes catapulted up his face with something like hope gleaming at their center. The river was loud in his ears. He could no longer hear what Tank was saying. By the look of it, though, even Tank seemed to recognize the astonishing brilliance of the moment, given the strange look on his face as he stepped off the tracks and away from Sully.

And it wasn't just Tank. Behind the big bully, Ox put his hand over his mouth while Dodger jumped around, waving his arms in a crisscross motion and yelling something Sully couldn't make out.

Maybe Tank is right, Sully thought, as he took another step back. Maybe that's the secret, after all. I just have to stick up for myself. Well, here I go. Just watch me. Sticking up for myself. Showing some self-respect.

Ox and Dodger crowded by Tank's side. Now all three of them were making wild gestures. Tank shook his head and pointed more forcefully at Sully. Dodger kept up the crisscross arm motion thing, while Ox cupped his mouth and bellowed something. He then pointed to the river on Sully's left. It was like having his own personal cheerleading squad.

Sully found himself amazed and relieved. Can this really be happening? Can it really be this simple?

He didn't have the nerve to retrace his steps and actually face them, but he was halfway to freedom. Tank had asked him what he was made of and he'd shown them. All he had to do was take another five or six steps to reach the other side of the river, and he'd already have proven to himself, and to them, that he had the courage to do this. It was all downhill from now.

The incredible bonus was that he no longer had to do it backward. With Tank, Ox, and Dodger cheering him on with their shouts and arm movements, and the sweet sound of triumph seeming to actually toll like a victory bell in his ears, Sully pivoted his body so he was now facing in the direction that freedom lay.

That was the moment he realized a train was heading straight toward him.

CHAPTER 36

The train horn drowned out every other sound: the insistent crossing bell, the vibration of the rails, the thudding of Sully's heart. Midway through a hasty step backward, Sully realized such a passive effort wasn't going to cut it.

He spun toward Tank, Ox, and Dodger, and suddenly understood what their gestures had really meant. He forced himself forward at top speed and landed hard on his knees. His misplaced eyes locked with the water beneath him as he clutched the tie in front.

The rails vibrated, the bridge shook, the train horn blasted with an increasingly panicked tone.

Sully realized he had only one option.

Before he hit the water, the steel wheels sliced over the space he'd inhabited just seconds before. The river gulped him up. Sully found himself suspended in a vacuum of sight and sound where nothing seemed to exist. Not even himself.

He thrashed his arms and legs in the frigid water, but neither struck bottom. Nor could he determine, at first, which way was up. It was like swimming through cold mud. Already his fingers were brittle as sticks and his clothes like hundred-pound weights.

The water rushed rather than drifted here. It carried Sully downstream, so that when he surfaced, Tank and the others were mere inches tall, huddled and posed like Eva's dolls on the hillside, watching him.

It didn't take much to make it to shore once Sully put some effort into it. He hauled himself onto the riverbank and breathed in the river stink, as he dragged his long hair out of his face.

He glanced over at the trio again. Their huddle had become a brawl. Tank shoved Dodger backward and Ox made a fist. It was Dodger who stepped away first to see that Sully had made it to shore. When the other two joined him, their stances visibly relaxed and they slapped each other's backs.

While Sully didn't believe they'd planned the train encounter, the way he'd escaped would surely be fuel for their fire, given that it hadn't actually killed him.

The wind bit into Sully's arms as he pulled himself up through the bushes. From this side of the tracks, his distance home was tripled.

Sully trudged home under gray skies. His teeth chattered on his left temple, loosening gobs of snot from his nose, which had hiked to his forehead. Cowering on his right cheekbone, his eyes squinted back tears but, for the first time, his maelstrom of emotions made room for something more than fear and sadness and loneliness. It felt a lot like anger.

CHAPTER 37

"A hundred and three." Mom pulled the thermometer out of Sully's mouth. "I'm sorry for doubting you, Sullivan."

Sully lay back in bed and closed his eyes. Something good had come out of the rail bridge incident after all. He hadn't actually told Mom what happened. If he told her about the rail bridge, he'd have to admit to skipping school. One problem at a time.

"Stay home tomorrow, and we'll talk about the rest of it when you're up to it, okay?"

"Thanks, Mom."

Sully smiled. A fever ought to be good for at least two days at home, and then it would be the weekend.

"Hey, Rooster." Eva put a hand on Sully's head like a mini-Mom.

"Don't you have a bus to catch?"

"It's after school, Silly."

Sully sat up and looked at his clock. His head throbbed and he felt cold and hot at the same time.

He trudged down to the kitchen and was rummaging in the medicine cupboard when the doorbell rang.

"It's not Halloween, yet." Eva stood at the front door. "What are you supposed to be, anyway?"

Wearing only his boxers, Sully snuck past Eva on his way upstairs.

"There are some people at the door for you, Rooster," Eva called.

Sully froze on the first step. What if Tank was home-delivering the Black Spot?

"One of them says he's Morty." Eva opened the door wider. "But I don't think so."

Sully grabbed the railing and hoisted himself up three steps when a voice called through the door.

"Dude, you okay?"

"We've brought you some homework, Bee Boy."

"Bee Boy?" said Eva.

Sully let out the breath he'd been holding.

"Tell them I'm sleeping," he whispered.

"We can see you, you know." Blossom pointed to Sully's reflection in the hall mirror.

"We heard rumors of something happening at the rail bridge, Dude."

"Keep it down." Sully raced for the doorway. "I don't want my sister to hear."

"We're here to help you, Dude."

"Look," said Sully, "I know you're trying to help, but it's not helpful. You wanted to help yesterday, too, and I nearly got run over by a train."

"That's not fair and you know it. How were we supposed to help when we didn't even know where you were? You're the one who ran off on us." Blossom's delicate, pale wildflowers had been replaced by deep purple lilies and black-eyed Susans that climbed the contour of her cheeks, accented with a web of dark green leaves. "And while we're at it, you can't really be so thick as to think we had anything to do with that video."

"No," said Sully. "I'm sorry for thinking that. But that's my point. How is it, exactly, that you think you're going to help me? You were right there with me Monday and look what happened. In a moment of weakness, I told myself that hanging out with you two might make me invisible. You know, take the focus off me? But it just made me a bigger target."

Morsixx jerked back a foot as if blasted with a pocket

of air, while Blossom's lilies piled up in the middle of her forehead.

"That's harsh, Dude."

"It's more than harsh," said Blossom. "It's extremely rude and insensitive. And if you look at the facts, you didn't do any better on your own. Arguably, you did worse. At least when you were with us, it was only your emotions at risk, not your life."

"Only my emotions," said Sully. "Yah. They don't matter at all."

"Believe me, you can learn to swallow your emotions when you have to," said Blossom. "You'd be surprised at how resilient the human spirit can be. But physical bullying is another matter, if the one taking it out on you is physically stronger."

Her eyes were like thorns pressing into his skull as she said this. Her fists balled at her sides as if ready to punch someone herself.

"There's strength in numbers, Dude." Morsixx reached for Sully's arm. "You need help, and we'll—"

"I'll take my chances on my own," said Sully. "And I'm sorry. I wasn't trying to be insulting. What I meant is that with the way you guys dress, you just kind of, you know, stand out. So people wouldn't notice me."

Blossom unclenched her fists and raised the fingers of her right hand to trace the yellow flowers on her cheek.

"You know our 'Shalott' essay is due Monday," she said. Though the comment was clearly directed at Sully, Blossom's gaze fell somewhere in between them, as if she were two different people operating within one body. "Even if you insist on refusing our help, you and I need to get together to work on it."

"Some stupid essay is not at the top of my list right now. If you really want to help me, do it for me."

"You are so messed up, Dude. You can't keep running."

"Watch me."

"I'm telling you, you don't have to deal with this on your own, Dude. We'll stick by you."

"You don't deserve loyal friends like us," said Blossom, "but nor do you deserve to be bullied. We'll go to the school administration together and stop it at the source."

"I already kind of burned that bridge," said Sully. "Look, I was out of line. I'm sorry. I know it's not your fault, and I also know what a jerk I'm being. But guys, I'm actually on the short list! I appreciate what you're trying to do, but please don't come to my house again."

Sully took a step back and pushed the door to close it, but Blossom shot her foot out to block it.

"Call me and we'll do this over the phone." She pushed a sheaf of paper into Sully's hands. "That's my number at the top. If you want to get credit for this essay, you'll have to do some of the work."

"I'm sick." Sully shoved Blossom's foot out of the way and shut the door. "I have to go."

CHAPTER 38

The rail bridge incident bought him two days. Three, if you counted the actual day it happened, but Sully's fever was normal going into the weekend. He had his talk with Mom and convinced her his mention of lists was just feverish confusion on his part, and explained away the "incidents" as male adolescent antics he assured her wouldn't be repeated. All this left him with no other option than to head to school on Monday morning.

So here he was, in Sex Ed again, but mercifully the class passed uneventfully. Tank sat at the back of the class and largely ignored him.

English was a different matter.

"Place your essays in the tray," instructed Wippet, as the class filed in. "I hope none of you has forgotten that a late essay will earn you a zero, and this paper is worth fifteen percent of your mark."

"I swear we have ours done," said a girl who frantically riffled through her knapsack.

"Didn't you print it off?" said her partner. "You said you'd bring it!"

"Ms. Wippet," the first girl protested. "We honestly have it done! I must have left it at home."

"Just get it in to me by the end of the day," said Wippet. "I'll be in my classroom until five." Sully looked around the room as Wippet launched into the lesson. Blossom hadn't arrived yet.

A half-hour into the lesson, with the seat still empty beside him, he pulled out the notes Blossom had shoved at him through the door last Thursday and found her number at the top of the page. Tuning out Wippet, he sent Blossom a message demanding to know where their essay was.

After another three-quarters of an hour, Sully punched "send" on his thirteenth irate message, since Blossom still hadn't responded.

"I'm certain that you have an excellent reason for launching missives to the outside world in my class." Wippet had somehow managed to sneak up on Sully's left and hovered over his shoulder. "Can you share with me what's so vastly urgent that it can't wait until lunch."

"I think he missed his train," said Dodger.

Wippet gave Dodger a strange look, but the rest of the class laughed.

"This is between me and Sullivan," she said. "Quiet, please."

Sully was relieved that she'd called off the rabid dogs, but it wasn't enough to put Wippet herself off.

"Show me, please." Sully reluctantly turned his phone so Wippet could read his last message.

"So, I take it your essay isn't among the ones on my desk," she said quietly. "That's a bit of a problem. And if I'm reading your message correctly, I think there might be more than a zero at stake here. Speak to me after class."

Sully approached Wippet's desk after the last student had left. His eyes circled his head while his ears pivoted his mouth.

"As I've said, if what I'm surmising about your role in developing this paper is correct, we might be talking about more than a zero grade," said Wippet.

While Sully didn't know exactly what Wippet was driving at, a glimmer of hope squeaked between her words.

A suspension, he thought. Why hadn't he thought of that before? A way to stay home legitimately until after one of the other two got the Black Spot was pure genius.

"While technically grounds for suspension," said Wippet, apparently reading Sully's mind, "removing you from school would help no one."

Beg to differ, thought Sully.

"Instead, Sullivan, I'm offering you remedial help. Additional classes."

"Wait, what?"

"Early morning and after school tutoring. More school, Sullivan, not less school. More school, to get you up to speed. No one gets left behind in my class. I'm willing to put in the extra time to ensure that. Are you?"

"I've got till five o'clock, right?" Sully gulped. He might as well give *himself* the Black Spot if he had to spend more time in Tank's arena.

"That's hardly the point, Sullivan. Do you understand that I'm trying to help you?"

"It's like that other girl said," Sully said. "The one who forgot her essay. That's the same with me. I was sick when Blossom and I worked on it and that must be why she's away today. She must have got what I got."

Wow, he thought. *Really quick thinking on my part.*

"But I'll go get it ... the paper we worked so hard on *together*. I'll get it to you by the end of the day."

"I will give you until the end of the day, Sullivan, but I can't help but notice you're struggling. And not just with the work, am I right?"

Sully feigned interest but his brain was racing.

"You can ask for help, you know. We're not the enemy. Maybe we don't always get it right, but I'd like to try. I've already spoken with Ms. Hamada. No one would have to know if you're worried about that."

No way, thought Sully. He believed Wippet was sincere, but she obviously didn't really get how things worked.

"Everything's fine," he said. "Really."

"You don't have to decide right away, but I want you to think about it, Sullivan."

"I'll just go grab the essay and be back by five. But, thank you."

Ms. Wippet nodded and gave him a concerned smile. "See you by five, then," she said.

With a sigh of relief, Sully dashed out of the classroom.

Reverse searching Blossom's number, Sully dug up her address and set out on foot to confront her at lunch.

CHAPTER 39

Sully imagined Despereaux Court would be fancy and regal looking, but the tiny houses on the small circle cried for paint, and their windows winked with mismatched cloth curtains. Number 27 hunched off to one side. Its shingles peeled up like dozens of little wings. Its porch knelt in a scrubby swath that might once have been a garden.

As Sully started up the dirt driveway, a scream exploded out the window before the screen door flattened against the side of the house. Blossom burst into the yard and grabbed the rail for support as she yelled back at the house.

"You have to stop!"

Turning to run down the driveway, she halted when she saw Sully. She clutched her hands by her mouth as lilies bled down her cheeks.

"Bee Boy? What are you ... why are ...?"

"Are you okay?"

"Who, me? Oh, that? Of course! Was I convincing?"

"What do you mean?"

"What do you think I mean? My acting! Did I convince you?"

"That was acting?"

"Don't be rude. I thought I was very good. I'm starring in a local theater production. It's why I missed school today. The first matinee is this Saturday, and I needed to practice my part."

"I thought you were going to look out for me," Sully said. "Our paper is due today. You said you'd handle it."

"I told you to call me." She sniffed and swiped the knuckles of one hand under her eyes, and then put her hands on her hips.

"I did try to reach you," Sully said. "About a thousand times this morning. Wippet's going to make me stay for extra classes if we don't hand it in by five. I don't need more exposure at school, understand?"

The sound of broken glass from inside the house was followed by what sounded like a wounded bear.

"Is everything okay?" Sully asked.

"Of course." Blossom looked back at the house.

"Thanks for helping me with my lines, Dad!" she called. "Listen, Bee Boy, can we go to your place?"

"What? Why?"

"To work on the essay, of course. I told you before, I won't do it for you. You're going to have to help."

"You're kidding me, right? Tell me you've got it done."

"It's all in here." She tapped her head. "C'mon, let's get going. You have a computer, right? I'll take the lead, but you'll have to add your two cents. If you pay attention and work hard, we'll get it to Wippet well before five."

"I'm a dead man," said Sully.

"Don't be so dramatic," Blossom said. The smeared lilies left angry pools of purple on the right side of her face and ugly blue blotches on her cheekbones.

"Wow," she said, catching Sully looking at her. "I must look a mess. Give me a minute."

She ducked between some trees beside the driveway. Dropping to her knees, she slid a rock to one side and pulled out a small wooden box that she opened to reveal dozens of markers and a mirror.

"We're kind of in a hurry," said Sully.

"I'll just be a sec. You really want to walk through the streets with an actress out of makeup?"

"My life is kind of at stake here," said Sully.

In less than a minute, Blossom emerged with black and red roses scaling her cheeks amidst dangerous thorns.

"Why do you do that?" Sully asked.

Blossom marched ahead of him, forcing Sully to trot to keep up.

"It's a memorial for my mother," Blossom said. "You know, like those roadside memorials?"

"Wouldn't it be easier to just carry a photo?"

"I don't forget what she looks like," Blossom said. "It's to remind me of what our life was like when she was here."

"She was a gardener?"

"Don't be so literal. So, do you have any thoughts on our paper at all?"

"I've been kind of preoccupied."

"Look," said Blossom. "I'll bail you out on this one, as long as you stop shutting Morsixx and me out. You could learn a lot from him."

"Oh, please. You have no idea who Morty really is. I've known him since kindergarten. All this death and dying stuff is just a stupid act."

"I think you're the one who doesn't know him," said

Blossom. "Morsixx is like a burnt marshmallow. All dark and dangerous looking on the outside, but inside he's just a softy. He's very deep."

"Yah, that really inspires my confidence—having a marshmallow as my bodyguard."

"He *should* inspire you. I think he's very brave."

"If anyone catches me at home, I'm a dead man."

"Then we better be fast," said Blossom.

While Sully only got about thirty percent of what Blossom wrote, it was thirty percent more than he'd understood before they started.

"In a mirror image of the life Offred is forced to lead in artful imitation of someone else's world view," Blossom wrote in their concluding paragraph, *"the Lady of Shallot weaves art in imitation of real life. This fabrication blocks both women from accessing their true selves. In the same way that Offred steps into obscurity when she exits the Commander's house and steps into the back van, so the Lady of Shallot is effectively already dead when she leaves her tower and finds the boat beneath the willow. Grown half-sick of shadows as she is, the Lady faces Morton's fork. Both women must ultimately make a choice*

between the walls they're hiding behind, and real life,
even if it kills them."

"Morty's fork?" said Sully. "Did you make that up?"

"It's Morton's fork, and it just means two bad choices," said Blossom. "The Lady of Shalott is dead, no matter which decision she makes—dead in her soul if she doesn't face the world, and literally dead if she does."

"Whatever you say," said Sully.

"Come on," she said. "We'll hand it in together to Wippet after fourth, as long as you agree to walk home with me and Morsixx."

After handing the paper to Wippet, Sully started toward the exit.

"Not so fast, Bee Boy." Blossom grabbed his arm. "We had a deal."

"Look, Blossom, I appreciate you bailing me out on this essay, but I've really thought about this, okay? We can hang out when all of this is over, and I'd actually like to do that. But in the interim, I need to disappear."

"No," she said. "That's not going to happen. You're obviously not thinking clearly enough to know what's good for you and I'm not going to stand by and let you hang yourself."

"Dude." As Morsixx walked toward them, his eyes darted from one to the other. "What's up?"

"I don't have time for this." Sully scanned the hall around them.

"Chill, Dude. We've got your back."

Eying the space between Blossom and Morsixx to plot his escape, Sully saw someone dart behind the bank of lockers in a suspicious move.

Sully stiffened and took a step back, but as the head bobbed out again, he realized it was only Winston, whose tragic and accusing eyes made it clear he hadn't forgotten Sully's unkind words in the parking lot the week before.

"I'm sorry, Winston," said Sully. He broke from Morsixx and Blossom to head home.

"Hey, Sally! I just heard! Congratulations!"

Dodger grinned when he strode up to the group. He grabbed Sully's hand and shook it.

"Really!" he said, as he backed away. "Congratulations!"

"What was that about?" said Blossom.

Sully's hand hung in the air in front him as he watched Dodger skip backward. Puzzled, he stared at his hand for a few seconds before he realized what had just happened.

A dot of black ink, about the size of a dime, stared back at him from the middle of his palm.

CHAPTER 40

"Bella, I'm sorry."

Sully's eyes fluttered open on the side of his face to see Winston kneeling over him.

"I'm not really mad at you, Bella. It's okay."

A circle of students, three bodies deep, peered down at Sully. The ones in the back popped up and down like jack-in-the-boxes to get a better view. The floor was hard beneath his cheek and something cold dripped from his nose into his ears.

"Need a tampon, TK?" someone said.

"Forget that," said someone else. "Look at his hand!"

Sully rolled onto his back and folded his hands together on his chest. It seemed safer to look at their feet.

"Show's over." Morsixx's black laced boots squared themselves inches from Sully's eyes. "Give me your hand, Dude. Let's go."

"You should all be ashamed." The purple lace-ups could only belong to Blossom. "This could be any of you!"

She grabbed Sully's hand and scrubbed at the Black Spot with her skirt.

"You heard him," Blossom commanded. "Show's over."

"What happened to your hand?" said Winston. "Are you hurt, Bella?"

"It's nothing, Winston," said Blossom. "See? It's all gone. Why don't you help us?"

Sully stumbled between the three of them as they pushed through the crowd and marched outside. As he looked at the gray blotch on his hand, still visible despite Blossom's efforts, more black spots began to form before his eyes.

"It's not going to happen, Dude," said Morsixx. "One of us will be with you at all times."

Sully looked from Morsixx to Blossom and shook his head.

"Don't you dare underestimate me," she said, touching her cheek. "Just don't."

"What's not going to happen?" said Winston.

"It's like a game, Winston." Blossom put her arm around Winston's shoulders. "Someone's trying to trick Sully, and we're not going to let them."

"Who's Sully?" said Winston.

Sully groaned. "This can't be happening."

"I told you. It's not going to happen, Dude. We're smarter than they are."

"There's my mom," said Winston. "Can we play the game again tomorrow?"

"Of course we will," said Blossom. "We're counting on you, Winston."

"We've missed the bus," said Morsixx, "but they're not coming after you today."

"You don't know that," said Sully. "Just because you want to help me doesn't mean you can."

"They won't attack today," Morsixx said again. "Half the fun for them is watching you sweat. They'll want to prolong that a bit."

"Gee, thanks, Morsixx. That makes me feel so much better."

"No, he's right," said Blossom. "The end of what those two other boys suffered was horrible, but it's the mental scars that don't heal."

"I'm so glad you two are experts, but you're not making anything better," said Sully. "I'm going to have to tell my mom."

"Do that, Dude. She's pretty fierce."

"With respect, do you really think involving your mom is going to make you less of a target?" said Blossom.

Exactly Sully's train of thought, but now he didn't know what else to do.

"In hand-to-hand combat against Tank, I'd put my money on his mom." Morsixx smiled. "Seriously."

"I don't know," said Blossom. "Adults are just as messed up as we are. More, in fact. This is something we have to fight ourselves. That's how it works."

"They can't touch you on school property, Dude. I can take Tank."

"Three of them, three of us," said Blossom.

The trio circumvented the park, which almost doubled the walk home. Blossom and Morsixx rattled off a number of rules, all to the end of not leaving Sully exposed. Both insisted on seeing him to and from his door each day. If the last two years were any indication, the attack wouldn't happen in daylight but, pretty soon, hours of darkness would outnumber hours of daylight by two to one.

"How adorable," said Blossom as they crossed over True Street. "Whose house is that?"

"Adorable isn't the word I'd use," said Sully. "Can we just get going?"

But Blossom had already approached the fence.

"Just give me a sec," said Blossom. "Wow, I love it!"

"A strange old man named Mr. C. lives there," said Sully. "As in really old, and really strange. He gets up in the dark and moves those figures around. It's sad and creepy."

"Mr. See ... as in 'I see you?'" said Morsixx.

"There's nothing sad about it," said Blossom. "It's actually fascinating. A visual story. Look ... Sleeping Beauty hand-in-hand with Charlie Brown, Pumbaa, and Lancelot. Look at all the flowers he's drawn on Sleeping Beauty's dress." She held up her arm and glanced at her own sketched flowers. "And Lancelot's the Red Cross knight the Lady of Shalott died for, Bee Boy. How coincidental is that?"

Sully saw Morsixx gazing at Blossom with a silly smile on his face.

"More like 'see' as in Senile," said Sully. "He thinks he's a wizard or a fortune teller or something. Can we go? I feel kind of exposed out here."

Blossom ran her finger along the little hole in the middle of the Madonna figurine and the weird black pack glued to her back, and then looked up at the house.

"Interesting," she said, indicating Darth Vader and the others before joining Sully and Morsixx as they walked toward Perdu. "Well, there's nothing random about it, that's for sure. There's a very clear good-versus-evil dynamic playing out there."

Sully glanced back at the Madonna figurine as they rounded the corner.

"Talk about crazy old people." Sully motioned two blocks up.

The Purse Lady shuffled toward them, bent at the waist, scanning the sidewalk from side to side.

"Trust me," Sully said. "Don't make eye contact."

"Poor thing," said Blossom. "What is she looking for?"

"I know who she is," said Morsixx. "She's not really old. I mean, not like fifty or anything. Her son was killed on this road. He was little."

"Killed? As in murdered?" said Blossom.

"No, hit by a car," said Morsixx. "My mom said he chased his ball into the street. She was with him, but it happened too fast."

"Your mom was with him?" said Sully.

"No, Dude. Not *my* mom; *his* mom. Her," he said pointing. "She hasn't been right since."

"You're telling me," said Sully. "I think she carries a Walmart store in that purse of hers."

"Have a little compassion, Bee Boy."

"Will you stop calling me that?"

"Will you stop acting like that?" said Blossom. "Honestly, it's like you think you're the only person in the world sometimes. Most times in fact. Did it ever occur to you that the rest of us have things we have to deal with, too?"

"Not like what I'm going through," Sully said.

He glanced up the street at the Purse Lady, and then back at Morsixx and Blossom. The Purse Lady had lost a son. Blossom had lost her mother.

"Sorry," he said. "No, you're right. I shouldn't have said that."

"Congratulations," said Blossom. "Maybe you have some human bones in you after all."

"Dude." Morsixx touched Sully's shoulder and pointed down his street.

Sully's mom was out in the driveway, talking to a boy.

It was Dodger.

CHAPTER 41

Sully hid with Morsixx and Blossom behind some trees and watched as Dodger helped Mom to the front door with some groceries. As he walked down the driveway and off in the other direction, Dodger turned and winked in Sully's direction.

"What are you doing?" Sully ran up to his mom as she put her key in the door.

"Oh, hi, Sullivan," she said. "Can you help me in with these?"

"Mom, why were you talking to Dodger?"

"You mean the boy who was just here? He said he was a friend of yours from school. He saw me struggling with the bags and offered his help."

"He's not a friend of mine," said Sully.

"Well, he spoke highly of you," said Mom. "Maybe you should get to know him better. Friends could help you settle in and feel better about high school."

"I already have friends." Sully nodded toward Morsixx and Blossom, who still stood across the street.

Mom's brow furrowed. "Sully, you know it matters *who* your friends are. That boy looks like a biker with all his skulls and chains. And does that girl actually have tattoos on her face?"

"Looks can be deceiving, Mom. Morsixx and Blossom are good friends."

"Morsixx? Blossom?" The crease in Mom's brow deepened. "Are these the friends you skipped class with last week?"

"Well ..." Sully faltered and flashed back to the first rail bridge incident, before the cafeteria video. "It wasn't really like that."

Mom swallowed, clearly unconvinced. "I think we have more talking to do, Sullivan. Give me some time to think and we'll sit down later, okay?"

"Tank is smarter than I gave him credit for, sending Dodger in like that," said Blossom. "You still think your mom's going to save you?"

"I pretty well know how that conversation's going to go," said Sully. "And I think I may have made it even worse."

"I kind of hate how clever he is," said Blossom. "It'd be easier to outsmart him if he were stupid, but he's definitely not. He's actually pretty strategic. Do you know he would have been in Grade 9 himself when he strung up that first boy? Obviously, an attempt to deflect any—"

"Geez, are you and Morsixx secretly in love with the guy? That's exactly what Morsixx said to me the first day of school. Who cares how smart he is?"

Blossom cocked her head at Morsixx and smiled. Morsixx blushed.

"Hello?" said Sully.

Blossom pulled her eyes back to Sully and linked one arm through his. "Know thine enemy is all, Bee Boy."

"Three of them, three of us, Dude." Morsixx patted Sully's back, but he was looking at Blossom. "We can hold it together for thirteen days."

"I've been giving this a lot of thought, Sullivan," said Mom at dinner. "I wanted to let you make your own way, but I think it's time I intervened. That young man from your school—"

"You mean Dodger? Mom, listen—"

"I don't recall his name," said Mom. "And, no, you

listen first, Sullivan. He told me he's on the Homecoming planning committee, and that's just the kind of thing you need to get involved in. It will expose you to a whole new circle of friends. I spoke to your homeroom teacher, Mr. Green, an hour ago, and he'll expect you at the meeting at seven o'clock, before school tomorrow morning."

"Mom, you're—"

"Sullivan, please. Don't fight me on this. I need you to give it a chance. This is for your own good. Homecoming is only a week and a half away, and I had to make special arrangements for you to join the committee at this late date. Mr. Green's expecting you at the seven o'clock meeting tomorrow morning. Both Bill and I have early meetings, so you're going to have to walk. So, eat up and get to bed early, because six o'clock comes early ... especially this time of year when it's still dark."

CHAPTER 42

"You are going to owe us for this when it's over, Dude."

"So, go back home to bed. Nobody's twisting your arm."

"It's cool, Dude. No worries."

"Easy for you to say."

"Well ... I, for one, think it's brilliant to be up this early," said Blossom. "Look at how beautiful that sky is."

"And look at how dark those shadows are," said Sully. "Tank and his gang manipulated my own mother into selling me out."

"In her own way, I think she really was trying to help you," said Blossom. "And, anyway, Tank isn't going to attack at this time of day."

"How do you know?"

"Well, for one, there's not enough time," she said. "It's already six-fifteen. By the time he snared you and strung you up—"

"Stop talking like that," said Sully.

"I'm just stating facts," Blossom said. "By the time he had it done, it would be broad daylight and he'd be caught red-handed. Besides, whether he's actually on the committee or not, it sounds like Dodger is, and Tank won't launch anything without him."

"There probably isn't even a meeting," said Sully. The thought had just occurred to him. "Who's on this committee, anyway? Maybe this was just a trick to get me to school, in the dark, before anyone else was around."

The hysteria bloomed in his chest like ink through water. "That's it. Think about it. This is probably going to happen this morning. On school grounds. Let's turn around and go somewhere else."

"Calm down, Dude. You said your mom talked to Green, right? Anyway, we're with you. We'll wait right outside."

"No, we won't," said Blossom.

Both Morsixx and Sully turned to look at her.

"We're joining the committee, too, Morsixx."

"We are?"

"Yes," she said. "We are. Aside from guarding Bee Boy—"

"Are you just trying to annoy me with that stupid name?"

"Sorry," she said. "Sully. Aside from guarding Sully, I'll bet the Homecoming committee could use a little independent thinking. What do you say?"

"I have a feeling our decorating sense might go a bit against the norm," said Morsixx.

"Exactly," said Blossom. "Besides, you know what they say: keep your friends close, and your enemies closer. This will give us an opportunity to keep an eye on Tank."

"Sally! Mortician. Buttercup." Dodger ushered them in as they hovered by the doorway. "Oh, goodie. New blood."

Green sat in a corner, marking papers. Tank lay across several desks in the back, sleeping, while Ox stood guard. Three Grade 10 girls comprised the rest of the committee. Sully pulled his gaze away from Tank and noticed their upraised eyebrows, as they scanned Blossom from head to toe, barely covering their smirks with the tips of their perfectly polished nails.

As he took his seat with his back to Tank, a sharp pain in the middle of Sully's chest made it difficult to breathe.

"So, like, we have our theme." Rebecca Smith tossed her head, so her Kardashian mane hung on the coquettish tilt of her face. "It's, like, brilliant, Tank. 'Disguise.' I love it."

"You two won't even need to dress up." Brittany Bell turned to Morsixx and Blossom. A slight, perky blonde with stylish short hair, her laugh was like one of those little Christmas bells.

"So, let's, like, make a list of decorations for the dance." Rebecca picked up some chalk and handed it to Cindy Leonni. Cindy's naturally curly shoulder-length brown hair looked considerably better on her than it did on Sully.

"Disguise is a pretty broad term," said Blossom. "Are we talking a spy theme? Halloween? Masquerade?"

"Just, you know, like, dress up." Rebecca turned to Mr. Green. "These questions are going to hold us back."

"I'm just saying that 'disguise' is a little vague," said Blossom. "If, as I suspect, you're thinking of those fancy sixteenth-century balls with the feathered masks and such, the term you're looking for is 'Masquerade.'"

"I wasn't looking for any term." Rebecca's dark eyes took on a nasty glint.

"It's okay, Rebecca," said Cindy. "I like the sound of Masquerade."

"Yah," said Brittany. "It sounds kind of like, you

know, mysterious. And sophisticated. I can totally see you in one of those little mask things, Rebecca."

Rebecca traced a sexy curve over the arch of one eye and tossed her hair again.

"Okay, so write that down, Cindy. Feathers and glitter. Maybe we should have some balloons and maybe some streamers, and—"

While Brittany and Rebecca huddled around Cindy, who transcribed their ideas onto the board, Blossom doodled with some markers on a scrap piece of paper. Within minutes, she walked to the front and set her drawing on the ledge beside the girls. With intricate detail, she'd sketched an elaborate scene with elegant archways and clandestine eyes, peacock feathers, and gauzy, exotic tents.

"Pretty cool," said Morsixx.

The three girls snatched up the drawing and gasped in unison.

"This is, like, totally what I was talking about," said Rebecca, her back to Blossom.

"Were you, like, eavesdropping?" Brittany glanced over her shoulder. "This is still our idea."

"Of course," said Blossom. She squeezed between Morsixx and Sully, a ghost of a smile in her eyes.

"Doesn't that bother you?" whispered Sully.

"You have a real gift." Morsixx touched her shoulder.

"They're not going to give you any credit," Sully said.

"Who says I want any?" said Blossom.

"But they stole from you," Sully insisted.

"You weren't too concerned about stealing credit for my essay."

Sully winced.

"I pick my battles," said Blossom. "I couldn't care less about this stupid dance. I'm just trying to keep you out of trouble."

"Okay, so you three are responsible for decorating the gym next Thursday at lunch," said Rebecca. "Make a list of what you need. You'll have an hour and a half before the pep rally starts."

"And don't you dare try to sabotage any of this with that disgusting sexist stuff you've been pulling." Cindy pointed at Sully.

"Who, me?" Sully's eyes slipped up to his forehead.

"Don't play innocent," said Rebecca.

"I'm with you," said Dodger. "That little display on the stairwell was really insulting."

"Just tell us when the next meeting is," said Blossom.

"Noon, Saturday," said Brittany. "After football

practice, so we can map out the pep rally and the crowning of the Queen."

Sully struggled to take a full breath.

"It's cool, Dude." Morsixx's voice was only loud enough for Sully to hear.

"Oh, and Sally," said Dodger, as the meeting broke up. "The guys and I are dying to know. What are you wearing to the Homecoming dance?"

CHAPTER 43

"Did you hear that?" Sully's voice maintained a perfect high C as he pitched his bag into the locker and grabbed his books. "It's happening at the Homecoming dance. In front of everyone. And with everyone wearing a mask ... thanks for that one, Blossom ... they've got the perfect cover."

"I'm afraid you're right," said Blossom. "Well, we'll just have to make the Masquerade theme work for us, too. If they don't know who you are, they can't harm you, right? And you'll believe me when I tell you I'm excellent at this kind of thing."

"Cool," said Morsixx. "We can make this work."

"No," said Sully. "I'm not going to be there. I'm forced to be on the committee, but they can't make me go to the dance."

"True," said Blossom, "but you remember that we're

the decorating team. We have to be there for that. You're going to be pretty exposed that day, like it or not."

"Yah, thanks for that, too," said Sully. Then, "Forget I said that. I know you're just trying to help."

"Good for you," said Blossom. "Keep exercising those human bones."

"Wait a minute," said Sully. "You can't even be there."

"Why not?" said Blossom.

"Your play," said Sully. "You said the play you're acting in was that day."

"What play?" Morsixx gave her that silly grin again. "I've been hanging out with an actress?"

"Oh," said Blossom. "That got canceled. We didn't sell enough tickets."

"How many more do you need to sell?" said Morsixx. "We'll come watch. I could probably get my mom to go, and I have lots of family who—"

"No, no, that's sweet," said Blossom. "It's not just tickets, actually. The lead actor got really sick. I just heard last night. He's going to be okay. We're just going to put it on in January, instead."

"Cool," said Morsixx. "What's the play?"

"Oh, it's just Shakespeare. You know, one of the comedies."

"That was a comedy?" said Sully. "The part I saw didn't look so funny."

None of this rang true to Sully. Was there even really a play in the first place?

But if there was no real play, what had Blossom been up to yesterday, Sully wondered. He'd have to think about this more when he had more time.

"You're being a little too literal," said Blossom. "There are many layers to both the comedies and tragedies. It's not like a sitcom or anything."

"Shakespeare's cool," said Morsixx. "Macbeth's witches showed up in some lyrics I'm working on."

"Lyrics, Morsixx?" said Sully. "So, you're a rock star now?"

"There's quite a bit you probably don't know about Morsixx," said Blossom. "Anyway, the thing is that we *will* be there on Saturday. Remember, know thine enemy. The more we know about the setup for the whole Homecoming event, the better."

CHAPTER 44

Sully derived unexpected comfort in knowing when the attack would occur. It was like cocooning in the eye of a storm. The hurricane was coming, but it wasn't coming yet. Still, it was concerning when Blossom failed to show up on Thursday, one week before the dance.

It was such a nice day, Sully and Morsixx decided to walk home rather than take the bus.

"Wait a sec." Morsixx dodged left onto True Street toward Mr. C.'s.

From Perdu, Sully saw him reach for one of the figurines that dangled in mid-air off the rail.

"What are you doing?" said Sully.

"Like Blossom said. The old Dude's kind of a poet or an artist. Just helping out."

He placed the Sleeping Beauty figurine back with the others, and then pulled his phone from his pocket.

"Blossom," he said, reading. "She just got up."

"She's lucky not to have a nagging mother on her back," said Sully.

"Wow, Dude."

"I'm an idiot," said Sully. "That was stupid."

"No argument there."

"I said I was sorry."

"Not till now you didn't."

"Anyway, is she sick or something?"

"Yah. She says she was up most of the night."

"Okay," said Sully. "I know how this is going to sound, but she's not too sick, is she? She'll be there Saturday, right?"

"You're right about how it sounds, Dude, but at least you know when you're being a jerk. I guess that counts for progress."

"It's just that this whole plan—"

"She said she'll be there tomorrow, Dude. Chill."

"Hey." Sully pointed at the fence where the Sleeping Beauty figurine had toppled over again. "Maybe you better stick to lyrics."

CHAPTER 45

Black spiky flowers, almost indistinguishable from the thorny vines, climbed out of the simple black dress that billowed like wings around Blossom on Friday morning.

"You two are starting to look alike," said Sully. "What's that supposed to be?"

He reached a finger out to touch a raised area on her left cheek, the only area with color. Blossom had shaded it to form the center of an elaborate, deep red flower, the petals of which wound around the back of her neck like tentacles.

"Like it?" She pulled her face away. "Don't touch. That one took work."

"Is that like wax or putty or something?"

"Family secret," said Blossom. "Anyway, I've been thinking about your disguise. What do you think about cutting your hair?"

Sully hugged the sides of his head and pushed his curtain of curls in front of his face.

"As in, short?"

"I haven't seen your face in two years, Dude. That could be interesting."

"Look who's talking," said Sully.

"Yes, as in short," said Blossom. "I'm good, but it's hard to miss all that hair, no matter how I dress you up."

"I don't know," said Sully.

"It's called hiding in plain sight," said Blossom. "You've got a few days to think about it, but the thing would be to cut it after the decorating, but before the dance."

At home that night, Sully stood in front of the mirror and pulled his hair away from his face.

No way, he thought. Even if his face wasn't as messed up as it was, his nose was too big, his eyes too small, and his ears stuck out a mile.

But the idea kept him awake. Expose himself to prevent being exposed. It was ridiculous. And it made a terrifying kind of sense.

CHAPTER 46

Sully, Blossom, and Morsixx huddled on the bleachers against the October wind. As the scrimmage ended, Rebecca corralled them to the first row, directing them with her pom poms as if they, too, were part of the cheerleading squad.

"The band will enter there." She pointed down the field.

Tank bumped Sully as he stepped up the bleachers to sit directly behind him. Assaulted by a waft of Tank's sweat, Sully's nose hid under his hairline and his ears cowered forward, so he only heard every third or fourth word.

"We were counting on a full moon to light our way to the dance after the game," said Cindy, "but the weather's not going to cooperate."

"So, we're going to put up a huge paper lantern at

the end of the field that we'll switch on the moment the Queen is crowned." Brittany smiled at Rebecca. "Dodger and Ox are going to take care of that for us."

Against his will, Sully's ears snuck to the back of his neck, seduced by a gruff whisper behind him.

"Are you getting this, Sally?"

Sully nudged Blossom, who sat between him and Morsixx, but she was explaining to Cindy that the cycle of the moon wasn't really considered weather.

"A full moon, Sally. Strung up over the end post. It'll be the best yet."

It was abundantly clear to Sully that the full moon Tank was talking about would not be made of paper.

"Or should it be at the other end?" Tank leaned back and spoke these words out loud. "Which do you think would be visible to more people, Sally? You should have some say in this."

"I don't—"

"Which would give the best exposure," Tank interrupted, "... be the most memorable?"

"What are you asking him for?" said Rebecca. "We're using this end post because it's closest to the gym."

"Works for me," said Tank. "Dodger, got it covered?"

"You know I do," said Dodger.

CHAPTER 47

"I'm going to vote for you, Bella."

Winston bounced on the balls of his feet. He waved a piece of paper and grinned as Sully, Morsixx, and Blossom made for the locker.

"Hi, Winston."

"What's the matter, Bella. Aren't you happy? Why aren't you happy?"

Sully's sleepless weekend had followed him to school. It pressed on his shoulders and weighed down his legs. His eyes peered out of deep wells in the middle of his face, and the corners of his mouth tugged at his nostrils, which, in turn, pulled at his scalp.

"Just a little tired, Winston."

"Like when you can't sleep the night before your birthday, right, Bella? I get it. You must be so excited."

"I've about had it." Blossom ripped a piece of paper

off Sully's locker. She'd flattened last week's prominent red flower and redrawn the petals so they snaked around her eyes. The spiky black flowers, crushed under sinister thorns, wilted on her cheeks. "This is too much."

"Don't worry, Dude." Morsixx yanked another piece of paper from a neighboring locker. "We'll have them all down before first bell."

"Have what down?" Sully yawned and then squeezed his eyes shut. He blinked a few times to clear his vision.

"They're just trying to psych you out. Don't worry."

"It's more than that," said Blossom. She crumpled the paper into a ball and then snatched another off an adjacent locker. "This is a ploy to ensure you attend the pep rally where they'll crown the Queen. And it's not going to work."

Sully rubbed his eyes and registered for the first time that the same flyer hung from every other locker. In the middle was a photo of his own face under the caption: *Our Next Homecoming Queen?*

"You don't want to be the Queen?" Winston cocked his head. He looked from Sully to the flyer in his hand, and back again.

"Do you remember what we said about someone trying to play a trick?" Blossom took Winston's hand.

"Morsixx, you work with Sully here. Winston and I will cover the west wing."

"Who's Sully?" Winston looked over his shoulder as Blossom steered him through the atrium.

Despite their efforts, residual flyers and digital reproductions chased Sully throughout the day.

"I knew we shouldn't have let you on the committee." Rebecca collared Sully between Sex Ed and English. "You're making a mockery of this, and I won't stand for it."

"Rebecca is going to be Homecoming Queen," said Brittany, who walked up beside them. "Make no mistake about it."

"If you and your creepy little friends try pulling something with the decorations on Thursday, we won't be responsible for what happens to you." Cindy stepped on Sully's foot with her nose inches from his ear.

"Well," said Rebecca. "Speak. What do you have to say for yourself?"

"We demand to know what's going on," said Brittany.

"You will answer to us in the end, so you might as well talk now," said Cindy.

The trio circled like Macbeth's witches. Sully eyes bounced between them, and his mouth worked hard around his tongue to form a response.

"Even you can't be stupid enough to think Sully had anything to do with this." Blossom swept into the circle. She grabbed Rebecca's hand from where it gripped Sully's shirt and held it between them. The wilted flowers on her face crushed together.

"Come on, girls." Rebecca yanked her hand away. "We're just wasting our time. The little witch is right. He's too pathetic to have thought this up."

"Bold move, guyPad." Whoever said this punched Sully's shoulder as he and Blossom moved through the crowd on the way to English.

"You'd make one ugly Queen, TK," said someone else.

"Is your dress going to be made of little white wings?" someone else called.

"Ignore them." Blossom steered them to a less populated area.

"Easy for you to say." Sully grabbed her right shoulder for emphasis.

Blossom winced and pulled away. She held her arm where Sully had grabbed her.

"Blossom, I'm sorry. The stress is getting to me."

"Don't touch me." Her eyes flashed with anger. The line of her mouth was taut and unforgiving, and her free hand balled in a fist before her.

"I said I'm sorry. I didn't mean it."

She spread her fingers to clasp her forehead as she tipped her head forward.

"I don't know how many times you and Morsixx have to help me before I—"

"Oh, listen to me." She raised her head. "That was silly."

Her eyes scoured Sully's own for several seconds as she clasped her hands in front of her mouth.

"Are you okay?" Sully asked.

"Yes, of course," she said, smiling. "I just bruised my arm on a door frame this morning. You know me, always rushing from one place to another. But enough about me. You're right, Sully, it's not easy to ignore what's happening to you, but what choice do you have? Have you thought more about your hair?"

"Yah, I have," said Sully. "Look, I know you and Morsixx are only on this committee to help me, but we're making this too complicated. I'm just not going to show up on Thursday."

Second period bell cut him off. Blossom took his elbow and hurried him toward English.

"That's a short-term solution at best," she whispered, as Wippet commenced her lecture. "You can't hide forever."

"If I'm not there, they can't get me," he whispered back.

"You're not getting it," Blossom whispered. "You miss a beating one day, you'll just get it the next. Believe me. It's not going away."

"It's a pretty elaborate plan they've made," said Sully. "My bet is that if they can't find me, they save face by picking someone else."

"And I think you're delusional. There's nothing random about any of this. I like you, Sully, but you've made yourself the perfect target for this prank. I wish it weren't the case, but this isn't going away."

"I'm going to review the last few weeks in preparation for your term test this Thursday," said Wippet. "And mind that I'm fully aware that Homecoming festivities start after lunch on that day and that some of you may be tempted to skip. May I remind you that unless you have a doctor's note, failure to write this test will earn you a grade of zero, which will make it virtually impossible for some of you to pass this course."

Wait, what, Sully thought? This is like Morton's fork or whatever Blossom called it. Except, he reflected, his fork had three prongs: fail English or face Tank or cut his hair.

Sully pulled his hair in front of his face and imagined his features bared for all the school to see. Could he really hide in plain sight as Blossom suggested?

"Hey, Sally." Dodger placed one of the flyers on Sully's desk at the end of class. "If you're going to win, you'll definitely need more exposure than this."

CHAPTER 48

"The best defense is a good offense," said Blossom on the way to school the next morning.

The vines on her face overtook the wilted flowers now. Hand-painted drops of blood sprouted where the thorns seemed to actually press against her skin.

"Wow." Morsixx brought a hand up to her face. His finger hovered close to a spot of blood. "It all looks so real."

Blossom turned her cheek away from his finger. Her eyes were shiny as she opened them wide and took a breath.

Morsixx took a step back and reddened. The black around his eyes accentuated his horrified expression. "I wasn't trying to come on to—"

"Don't be silly." She grabbed his hand in both of hers. "It's not that. You're perfectly lovely."

"Did you just call Morsixx lovely?" Sully felt suddenly like the proverbial third wheel. "Wow," he said. "Do I feel stupid. I just got a nasty image thinking what your kids would look like. Like dead gardens."

"Just shut up, Dude."

"No, no," Sully said. "I'm not judging. That's cool. I'm about to be humiliated in front of the entire school, but you guys go about your little romance. Don't worry about me."

"No idea why you were singled out for the Black Spot, Dude. You're so likeable and all."

"Never mind, Morsixx." Blossom's brow furrowed over her flat eyes. "It's fine. Sully's right. We do need to focus on him. Now, as I was saying, the best defense is a good offense."

"I was out of line," said Sully. "The stress is making me such a jerk. I'm sorry."

"Just listen," said Blossom. "I have this worked out. Tank is expecting you to run. He's counting on it. But what if you turned the tables on him?"

"Like how?"

"Yesterday I said the whole Homecoming Queen thing was to make sure you showed up at the pep rally," she said. "But that's wrong. He's counting on you not showing up."

"But I have to come tomorrow. You heard what Wippet said."

"Yes, and Dodger will know that, of course," Blossom said. "My bet is he's expecting you to ditch either before or after the decorating. Assuming they manage to grab you, they'll keep you hidden for a while, and Tank has a perfect alibi since he'll be playing football. By the time the crowning ceremony starts, everyone will be in costume and it will be dark, and while everyone's focused on which girl is crowned Queen, Ox and Dodger will be stringing you up on the end post in preparation for the lighting of their stupid full moon. Except that the full moon will be your—"

"I got it, Blossom," said Sully.

"Sorry," said Blossom. "Anyway, the point is that since everyone will be in costume ... except you, who, theoretically, would have no clothes on at—"

"I said, I got it, Blossom."

"Well," she said. "Since everyone else will be in disguise, no one will be able to say for sure who did it."

"I won't let them take him," said Morsixx. "I don't pick fights, but if I need to defend something, I can and will. I'm a Bearheart. My ancestors know a thing or two about struggle."

"I have a lot of faith in you, Morsixx," Blossom said, "but think about it. They'll be anticipating that. You could stop one or two of them, but what if there are more than that?"

"You think there will be more of them?" said Sully.

"I don't think we can rule it out," said Blossom. "But the thing is, I think we have to take it from them. Outsmart them."

"Like how?" asked Sully.

"If you were on the battlefield, and your enemy had a knife to your throat, wouldn't you rather kill yourself?" she said.

"What? I'm not going to kill myself!"

"It's just an analogy," said Blossom. "My point is that your enemy is bent on exposing you in the most humiliating way possible. The best way for you to escape that is to do the exposing yourself. Put yourself in control."

"I'm hoping you just mean my hair," said Sully, "because I'm not—"

"Yes, your hair," said Blossom. "You see, the whole Homecoming Queen thing gave me an idea. The stupid decorations will only take us an hour. I'm going to use the last half-hour to transform you into the most beautiful Homecoming Queen candidate this school has ever seen."

"Cool," said Morsixx. "So, when we leave the gym at the end of lunch, we'll be able to walk right out of there and get him to safety. It will be like the Dude vanished."

"Exactly," said Blossom. "Except we're not going anywhere. You're going to stand up on that stage with all the other Queen candidates, where there's no way they'll be able to nab you."

"But didn't you say they'd just get me another day if I dodge the first bullet?"

"Yes, I did," said Blossom. "Which is why, when you get your opportunity to give your candidate speech, you're going to expose the whole deal in front of the entire school, administration included. You'll tell them you've been singled out. You'll tell them about the past attacks and name the antagonists. Morsixx and I will help you. We'll be right beside you. I've already started work on your speech that will sway the crowd to your side, and make it impossible for Tank to lay a finger on you ever again, because everyone will now know it was him."

"If it's really that simple," said Morsixx, "why don't we just go to the office and tell them all this now?"

"Because Sully has tried that," she said. "No. We need the mentality of a crowd to make this work."

"I don't know," said Sully. "Let me sleep on it."

Morsixx cocked his head and peered at Sully through a picture frame he made of his fingers. "You're going to make one ugly Queen, Dude."

CHAPTER 49

Wippet's back was to the students as Blossom drifted into class on Wednesday. With her arms folded across her stomach, Blossom stared straight ahead, zombie-like, and then eased carefully into her seat.

"Where were you this morning?" Sully whispered.

"Sorry," she said, without looking at him.

"Well, where were you? If I'm going to put my life in your hands, the least you could do is show up."

"I overslept," said Blossom. "I'm sorry."

"Well, you better not do that tomorrow," he said. "As terrifying as it is, I'm going to go along with your plan. I'm trusting you."

"I said I was sorry." She turned to face him.

"What have you done to yourself now?" He shrank back.

Apparently not content with photo-realism, she'd carved a depression in her lower lip to accentuate a thorn she'd drawn creeping out of her mouth.

"It's a story," she said. "Haven't you been following?"

"Not one I want to read."

"I'm not writing it for you."

"Seriously," said Sully. "You're overdoing the whole dead garden thing. What's next? Spring again?"

"Something like that."

As Wippet turned to face the class, Blossom shifted sideways away from Sully and opened her notebook. Bent low over the pages, she began making notes before the lecture even started.

"Earth to Blossom," Sully said at lunch.

"Human bones, Dude, remember?" said Morsixx, but Sully saw the concerned glance he gave Blossom as she stared into space while she feathered her little finger over the crevice on her lip.

"Everything cool, Blossom?" Morsixx said.

"To be honest," she said, "I'm not feeling great."

"As in sick?" Sully's voice did the octave thing again.

"Yes," she said. "As in sick. My stomach hurts and my head hurts."

"Maybe you shouldn't be here," said Morsixx. "I'll walk you home now if you like."

"And leave me here alone?" said Sully.

"You can come," said Morsixx. "We'll both walk you home, Blossom."

"No, it's okay," she said. "I don't want to go home. I can handle it."

"But you are going to be there tomorrow, right?" said Sully. "I don't mean to be insensitive, but—"

"I know," she said. "It just keeps happening by accident, right?"

"No, it's just that—"

"It's okay, Sully," she said. "I'll do my best."

"It's just tomorrow, and then you can rest all weekend, right?" said Sully. "I feel like a jerk, asking you when you're not feeling well, but it's not like you're on your deathbed or anything. Can't you just take some aspirin or something?"

"I might just do that," said Blossom. "Don't worry. I'm sure by tomorrow the pain will be a distant memory."

CHAPTER 50

Staring at his test paper on Thursday morning, Sully's pen hovered between four equally plausible multiple-choice answers. He frowned at the empty doorway for the hundredth time. Surely Blossom would come floating in any minute. The essay questions on page three might as well have been in some medieval dialect.

Blossom didn't come floating in.

With one eye on Dodger, he slipped his test into his backpack. Maybe he could convince Wippet after the fact that she'd lost his test, giving him a chance to rewrite it.

The hallway stretched like a minefield. Where was Morsixx? Had they both bailed on him? The best place to be now was out in the open, but eventually all the students would migrate outside to the football field and, within the noisy crowd, he'd be as good as dead.

With one hand on the railing, he moved his foot forward to take a step down the main stairway, when he felt the hot breath of a whisper on his neck. His eyes leapfrogged over each other to get a look at who was there. He bent his knees to brace himself and gripped the railing with both hands, determined not to surrender meekly.

"Where is she, Dude?"

Sully sank to sitting, with his heart hammering.

"Are you trying to give me a heart attack?"

"She didn't show up for the exam?"

"What does it look like?" said Sully. "How could she do this to me?"

"Just a thought, Dude, but maybe it has nothing to do with you."

"How sick can she really be, Morsixx? Couldn't she just take some aspirin or something?"

"I'm kind of worried about her," said Morsixx. "This isn't like Blossom at all. But we'll figure it out."

"How exactly are we going to figure it out, Morsixx? Blossom was kind of important to the plan."

"If she can't come to us, we'll go to her, Dude."

"Okay," said Sully. "Okay, you're right. Sorry. I know Blossom wouldn't abandon me. She's got to be really sick not to show up today."

"So, let's go to her place and figure out what to do next."

"You mean just waltz out the front door? Just like they expect?"

"Not like they expect," said Morsixx. "We're going to the gym first."

"What's that going to accomplish? They'll just be waiting for us when we're done. And, besides, I don't have a clue what we're supposed to build."

"They won't see you leaving, Dude."

"How are we going to manage that?"

"I have used scissors before, Dude."

CHAPTER 51

"I can't do it." Sully backed away from the blades in Morsixx's hand. "Having you butcher my hair would run a close second to the Niner itself."

"It's hard to help you, Dude."

"Would you let me cut your hair?"

"Again ... not the point, Dude. Tell me what you want to do?"

"Well, I can't stay here."

"So, put on some of that stuff. We'll reinvent you."

"What are you waiting for?" Rebecca poked her head in the door. "You guys better not screw this up. Where's the tattoo girl?"

"She didn't—" Sully began.

"... want to leave it to the last minute," said Morsixx. "She prepped some of it at home, and is just getting it from her locker."

"That's not—" Sully said.

"... the way we planned it," said Morsixx. "But Blossom assured us it would be better that way."

"Whatever," said Rebecca. "I trust her way more than you two, anyway. But I'm warning you. It better be perfect and it better be ready. And don't leave any mess behind."

"It won't even look like we were here," said Morsixx. "Just chill."

"Don't you chill me," said Rebecca. "I'm going to be back to check up on you in, like, half an hour."

"I repeat, Dude," said Morsixx after Rebecca closed the door. "It's hard to help you. You think that would have made things easier, to tell them Blossom didn't show?"

"I'm an idiot." Sully looked around the room. "Thanks for the save. I just feel so messed up these days." He took a deep breath. "Okay. So, we've got five or ten minutes max to come up with something and get out of here."

"Look over there," said Morsixx. "Somebody's uniform."

"There's got to be another way," Sully said, as Morsixx sized him up.

"Good thing you're short, Dude. I think we can make this work."

"It's freezing," said Sully as they ducked out the side door a few minutes later. "How do they wear something this short in this weather?"

"You really should have shaved your legs, Dude. You're hurting my eyes."

"Shut up." Sully held one of the pompoms at the top of his legs from the front. The other covered his butt. The high ponytail, created to camouflage his distinguishing mop of curls, flipped in the whipping wind, as Sully's lips side-swiped his eyes and swerved down his face to lodge in the crevice of the ear that hung onto the right side of his chin.

"Go on ahead, Dude," said Morsixx. "I'll keep you in sight."

"Bella? Bella! You look beautiful. Sort of."

"Winston, shhh," said Morsixx. "It's a secret, okay?"

"A secret?" said Winston.

"Like, how a bride doesn't want anyone to see her before she walks down the aisle," said Morsixx. "Like that kind of secret."

"That's not a wedding dress, Bella. Are you trying to trick me?"

"Well, it is kind of a game, Winston," said Morsixx. "Look, can you help us out? I want you to pretend you never saw us, okay? Especially Bella. Can you do that?"

"I'm good at secrets," said Winston. "I never even told Blossom's secret."

"That's great, Winston," said Sully. "We gotta go now, okay."

"What was Blossom's secret?" said Morsixx.

"About her shadow sickness." Winston clamped a hand over his mouth. "Oh! I didn't say that."

"Her shadow sickness?" said Morsixx.

"It's just a reference to something from our English class," said Sully. "You know how dramatic Blossom can be. Winston, we have to go. We'll see you later, okay?"

Winston's eyes were wide until Morsixx put an arm around his shoulder.

"It's okay, Winston." He drew an imaginary zipper across his lips and then gave him a thumbs up. "I won't tell on you. Just go have fun."

Taking a block's lead, Sully navigated a roundabout route to Blossom's. Drizzle oozed from the gray October sky. The landscape flattened perspective, as if the clock had leapt a few hours ahead, allowing dusk to step on noon's toes. It was the kind of sky where you saw things that weren't there, and didn't see things that were.

Surrounded by forest as it was, Despereaux Court was

darker still. Standing at the foot of Blossom's driveway, Sully jumped as the screen door slammed against the side of the house. He jumped again as Morsixx caught up with him and laid a hand on his shoulder.

"You might want to change before we knock." He pointed to Sully's backpack.

The screen door squeaked on its way closed, before the wind grabbed it again, flinging it wide to reveal the front door half-open, politely parted as if in the middle of a sentence.

"Strange weather to keep your door open in," said Morsixx.

"You knock while I go change." Sully started toward the wood.

"Wait," said Morsixx. "Do you hear that?"

As the wind took a breath, a low moan traveled down the driveway, chased by some heaving gasps. The screen door smacked the outside of the house again, and a shadow slumped across the open frame of the inside door.

"Something's not right," said Morsixx.

"Blossom?" called Sully.

The pair crossed the barren lawn and crept up the stairs, as the moan leaked through the open door.

Morsixx's knock pushed the door inward to reveal

a grizzled, middle-aged man sprawled in the hallway. Dressed only in boxers, some socks, and a stained, sleeveless undershirt, he slumped in a corner with a bottle clutched in one hand. His white skin was puffy and jaundiced. Deep pockets crouched under his bloodshot eyes.

"Sir?" said Morsixx. "Is Blossom here?"

"Maybe we shouldn't be here," said Sully.

"Sir." Morsixx took a step inside. "We're here to see Blossom."

The man turned his unsteady gaze to look at Morsixx.

"Are you Blossom's father?" Sully asked.

"Where's Blossom?" Morsixx demanded.

The man turned his face to the wall. His shoulders shook and a knot formed in Sully's stomach as he realized Blossom's father was weeping.

"Blossom?" Morsixx and Sully shouted the name together.

"I didn't mean to hurt her," her father said between sobs. "I didn't know what I was doing."

"Where is she?" Morsixx said. "Tell us where she is."

"I don't know," said her father. "I don't know. I'm sorry. Tell her I'm sorry."

"I'll search the house," Morsixx stepped over Blossom's

father and pushed into the kitchen. "You look outside."

Sully backed out of the house.

He circled the dilapidated house and then ventured off the driveway, remembering Blossom's stash of markers just inside the forest. Stumbling from rock to rock, he finally spied the flat rock he recognized as the lid to her secrets.

In the half-light, the contents looked unremarkable. Orderly, even. Lined up in perfect formation, her markers were tied together with a black ribbon. A small box held some photographs of a beautiful black woman—some of her alone, some with a younger, unpainted version of Blossom—beside which was a small glass bottle with a lock of dark hair in it. Underneath the bundle of markers was the hand mirror Sully had seen Blossom use. A crack down the middle fractured his image, but it was only when he read the words on the outside of a small white envelope propped against the box that he yelled for Morsixx.

CHAPTER 52

"Open it, Dude. Give it to me."

"I'm opening it," Sully's hand trembled. "It's addressed to both of us."

Inside was a single sheet of paper containing a dozen or so lines of poetry.

> On either side my doorway lies
> A different world with separate skies.
> The bottle drinks his desperate cries;
> The flowers are my thin disguise;
> Her shadow was our light.
> In place of memory only sorrow,
> Yesterday's light too dim to borrow.
> Four gray walls haunt each tomorrow.
> Her knight became the night.

My magic web with colors gay
Was meant to chase the dark away;
To give him space to find his way,
But ugly night claimed every day.
        Her shadow stole all light.
With dangerous fists he'd challenge why;
I can no longer keep the lie.
I am full-sick of shadows, I
        Surrender to the night.

"This is part of the poem we did our paper on, I think," said Sully. "But different."

"I don't like this, Dude. Something's really wrong."

Both of them looked up at the house through the pale-yellow woods.

"We have to find her," said Sully.

"The rail bridge," said Morsixx. "Remember what she said about that place? Like it was out of a poem?"

"Okay, yah," said Sully. "But I'm also thinking of Mr. C.'s fence. She said that was like a story, too."

"We have to pick," said Morsixx. "If we're thinking the same thing, we don't have time for a mistake."

"Or we split up," said Sully. "I'll take the fence."

"You know they may be out there looking for you."

"Don't even say that," said Sully.

"I won't say it, then, but you know it's true," said Morsixx.

"I'm going to have to risk it," Sully said. "I think Blossom might be in more trouble than I am. And I don't have time to change."

The rain stung his thighs as Sully cut across several backyards en route to Perdu. His hair, now loose from the ponytail, whipped forward with the wind. It lashed his eyes, which took cover beneath his nose.

"Did you find it?" The Purse Lady appeared out of nowhere. She grabbed his arm and searched his face.

"I'm sorry." Sully wrenched his arm away and dodged a car in his race for True Street. "I'm in a hurry."

The top rail of the fence, dislodged by the wind, speared the earth at a forty-five-degree angle. Darth Vader, Goyle, and The Riddler remained upright, perched near the end, as if ready to leap. Mud sucked at the other figurines, which were scattered like casualties on a battlefield. Sleeping Beauty floated toward the sidewalk crevice on a rivulet of rainwater.

Sully scanned the yard and across the street, at the sloping bank that crawled toward the black water of Fairy Lake. He looked back toward Perdu where the

Purse Lady slumped against a streetlight, and then back at the chaos of the fence.

His eyes crept out from beneath his nose and pulled his gaze back to the lake. As he crossed over True Street, he squinted through the branches of the quivering aspens, and beyond the broad branches of the towering oaks. As his feet reached the shore, his eyes bolted to the back of his neck and spied something mere yards behind him that caused him to duck and double back toward the house.

CHAPTER 53

It was Sully's long hair that ultimately betrayed him. For the last ten seconds, he had actually felt something like hope burning through his hammering fear. Tank was huge, but Sully's feet had managed impressive speed, thanks to all the walking he'd done over the last few weeks.

The sharp yank on his scalp instantly extinguished his fleeting belief in escape. At thirteen seconds, True Street cartwheeled over his head, as his neck snapped back and his feet became airborne.

At eighteen seconds, Tank's forehead inched into view, upside down and unfurrowing, as his eyes transitioned from anger to triumph. A combination of spit and sweat accelerated down his brow toward Sully's open mouth, which dodged behind his ears to avoid the inevitable.

Tank's beefy hand grabbed Sully's shoulder at twenty-two seconds, and spun him, so Sully now had a full vertical view of the last person he would see before he died.

CHAPTER 54

"Show time," said Tank.

Sully swung one fist and then the other, connecting with the side of Tank's skull on the third try. The hit succeeded only in causing Tank to narrow his eyes and frown.

"You're pathetic, Sally." He tossed Sully to the ground. "Almost not worth the effort."

Sully landed face down and clawed the mud in front of him. He managed half a yard before Tank's knee skewered him in place.

Sully's right cheek pressed against the cold earth, trapping his lips. In a narrow escape, his ears scuttled loose and climbed the other side of his face in time to feel Tank's hot breath as he pinned Sully's arms and leaned forward.

"Here's how it's going to go," Tank said.

Sully jack-knifed backward and his temple cracked back against Tank's face.

Owing to the fact that his eyes still sat on the back of his neck, he saw the spurt of blood from Tank's nose. He also saw Tank's fist rocket toward him in reaction, which enabled him to shift his head just enough to evade the blow.

"I can't do this right now," Sully said. "You have to let me go."

Tank laughed. "Not a convenient time for you?"

"No." said Sully. For once, his voice didn't roller-coaster out of control. "It's not. My friend's in trouble."

"Well, you two have something in common."

"I'm serious," said Sully. "We can't do this right now. You have to let me go."

"I'm serious, too," said Tank.

Sully's right fist still clenched the mud he'd grabbed in his first attempt at escape, as Tank dragged him to his feet. He opened his hand with the thought of flinging the mud at Tank's face, but realized something was lodged inside the dirt. As Tank dragged him across the street, Sully spread his fingers and watched the rain wash away the muck to reveal a small rainbow ball in the palm of his hand.

CHAPTER 55

Holding Sully with a single hand, Tank pulled out his phone with the other and pressed the screen.

"Where are you two idiots?" he said.

While Tank yelled various insults and commands into the phone, Sully tossed the little ball to the side and watched it roll between the roots of an ancient oak by the side of the lake.

"Move it," Tank said, before jamming the phone back in his pocket.

Sully twisted sideways and managed to squeeze out of Tank's headlock. He jabbed the bully with an elbow before lighting off down the slope toward the lake. He squinted through the rain, and tried to make sense of the object floating a dozen yards upstream, where Fairy Lake gentled around a curve.

"Let go of me," said Sully, as Tank grabbed the back

of the skimpy cheerleader T-shirt he still wore, the letters wfhs emblazoned across his chest.

"Shut up." Tank twisted Sully's arm behind his back.

"Ow!"

"I said, shut up." Tank grabbed Sully's other arm and tied his wrists together behind his back.

"Blossom needs me." Sully struggled as Tank dragged him back to the oak tree. "Let me go."

"Your begging is pathetic." Tank tossed Sully to the ground, so he could free a rope that was tied to a branch overhead.

"I'm *not* begging," said Sully. "I'm *demanding* you let me go right now. Just stop this."

Without the use of his arms, Sully stumbled to standing. Before he could take a step, Tank kicked his feet out from under him. The side of his head slammed into the ground, cutting his lip and bruising his cheek.

Hauled to his feet again, Sully swivelled sideways and then back, trying for a roundhouse kick to Tank's groin, but he succeeded only in landing on the ground again.

"Untie me!" Sully pushed to his knees again. "I mean it!"

"Do you want to know why I picked you, Sally?" Tank grabbed the front of Sully's shirt and ripped it up the middle. The taut neckline resisted and bit into Sully's neck until Tank slid a jackknife underneath to slice it open.

Cold rain pricked against Sully's bare chest. On his knees again, he coughed from the t-shirt's choke hold, and lifted a battered knee in another attempt to stand.

"I picked you because you're weak," said Tank.

Tank's face didn't hold amusement or even triumph. Sully struggled to name the emotion it held. Resignation? Frustration? Duty? Almost as if this were a chore he had to complete.

"So weak that you don't even know, yourself, who you are," said Tank. He flicked up his wrist so the knife split Sully's t-shirt at the shoulders, where it fell to the ground.

"None of that is important right now," said Sully.

"... and even though you'd do anything to save your pathetic self—"

"You're not listening to me! Blossom needs my help."

"... grovel in front of your enemies and betray your friends—"

"I get it. I'm worthless. But this isn't about me right now."

"Just shut up." Tank pushed Sully to the ground again. "The Niner is a public service. Weakness needs to be exposed, as my dear old dad is fond of saying. You chose yourself, Sally. You caused this."

As Tank wound the rope around his ankles, Sully lunged forward. He sunk his teeth into Tank's calf which earned him a kick in the head before he found himself dragged backward through the leaves.

"Now, let's get on with this." Tank pulled on the rope, so Sully was lifted upside down a foot above the ground.

He arched his back and thrashed forward in a futile attempt to knock Tank off his feet. "Let me go! My—"

"Quiet now, Sally." Tank placed his finger on Sully's lips.

As Sully swung from the branch, his skirt fell away from his legs to reveal his underwear.

Tank smiled. "I almost want to leave the skirt, Sally."

"Stop," Sully protested.

Tank slipped the tip of the knife under the waistband of Sully's underwear. As his arm flexed for the upward motion that would slice the garment up one side, Tank's face slackened and, for a few seconds, it was as if he were suspended in a pickling jar before he crumpled to the ground under Sully's head.

CHAPTER 56

"Go!" Mr. C. extended his flat palm level with Sully's eyes. Sleeping Beauty lay face down on Mr. C.'s hand, half-immersed in mud.

Looking down at Tank, Sully saw one of the green walnut pods lying inches from where he'd landed.

"Now, tuck and roll," said Mr. C.

"What?" said Sully.

Mr. C. pulled the bind off Sully's wrists and then sliced at the rope with the knife he'd fished out of Tank's slack hand. "I said, tuck and roll."

Gravity kicked in before Sully could react.

"I could have broken my neck!" He pushed himself up from Tank's solid girth, which had broken his fall.

"You could be hanging naked, stupid boy. Now go. You don't have much time."

Sully raced to the water's edge and squinted upstream

through the sleet. He wiped blood from his eyes, startled to find them two-thirds of the way up his face, exactly where they should be. Even on the right sides.

A flimsy rubber raft floated toward him from half a dozen yards away. The long white dress of its passenger trailed loosely, left and right, in the dark water. Sully didn't have to see her face to know it was Blossom. Her hands were folded like a corpse across her chest, and her long multi-colored hair hung lifelessly, rendered uniformly dark by the rain.

Sully shivered. The putrid smell of decaying vegetation stuck in his throat as he stepped into the lake. Icy brown water chewed at his ankles. The lake bottom sucked at his feet. While the river trundled moderately at this point, still two dozen yards from the falls, the raft halved the distance between them before Sully took a second step.

Another few steps and the tiny cheerleader skirt spread like petals around his waist. Picking up speed, the raft threatened to pass him if he didn't hurry.

Sully plunged forward and kept his eyes on Blossom, as the mucky bottom fell away. His mouth floated sideways from his cheek to land just above his chin as cold water gripped him round the middle and stole his breath.

The lake slapped Sully's face as a gust of wind plucked the raft out of reach. Foul water drove his nose up the middle of his face, dodging his mouth before settling.

Spluttering, gasping, dragging in breath, Sully kicked hard with his legs to make one last push. He grabbed the end of the raft and pulled himself even with Blossom's face, as the current tugged them forward.

Washed clean of gardens, her earth-brown complexion glowed in the dull light. Instead of flowers, ugly bruises bloomed on her face and arms. Her left eye bulged with swelling, and dried blood darkened the split on her lower lip.

Sully's ears sprinted to either side of his head and picked up the roar of the falls, now ten yards away. Using the raft as a flutter-board, he kicked hard for shore, but the wind and the current joined forces against him and tossed him backward. As the raft unbalanced, Blossom slipped into the water. Her head lolled sideways as her dress strained for the bottom of the lake.

Sully wrapped one arm around her waist and pushed her face above water. He pulled toward shore but, despite his best effort, lost three feet of distance toward the falls for every one he moved across the lake.

Eight yards from the drop, Sully spied a metal pipe

sticking a few inches above the water, which he knew to be anchored in place to spurt a decorative fountain on summer days. Since the wind buffeted him in that direction anyway, Sully gave in to the force, intent on grabbing the pipe to anchor them until they could be rescued.

The wind shoved him one way and then the other, causing Blossom's face to submerge. As Sully struggled to reorient himself, the wind yanked him back. The sharp metal sliced across his scalp and a wave of nausea seized him as he lifted Blossom's face above water and focused his eyes on the shore again.

Six yards from the falls, a distant voice reached him.

"Dude! Sully! Grab the rope!"

Four yards from the falls, Sully looked up to see Morsixx lying on the overhanging branch of the last enormous tree before the drop. His coal black hair hung over his face, and a noose dangled from his outstretched hand.

The lake ached to pull them forward. Numb and sluggish, Sully reached wildly, as he and Blossom floated under the branch. He grabbed the noose and pulled it over his head and shoulders, gasping as it cinched across his chest. No longer sure which way to go, he lost sight of land altogether as the water closed over their heads.

CHAPTER 57

The first time Sully woke, a cocoon of darkness enveloped him. Feeling his arms at his sides, he jerked them forward, grasping for Blossom in the murky water. Acute pressure stabbed in his right forearm, and a warm hand landed on his forehead.

The second time Sully woke, warm pressure encased his right hand. As car headlights illuminated the room from a window on the left, Sully turned his head in the direction of the warmth to see his mother sleeping in a chair by his bed. Her neck bent back at an awkward tilt. Her light snoring kept time with the passing cars. What was his mother doing in his room? It was beyond creepy.

The third time Sully woke, harsh light pressed on his eyelids, and a fist of pain hammered on the inside of his skull.

"Welcome back, Dude."

Sully opened his eyes to see a pale blue curtain partially surrounding his bed. An odor, vaguely poisonous yet vigorously clean, clung to the inside of his nostrils.

"Your mom just left to get coffee," said Morsixx. "You've been out a long time."

"Blossom—" said Sully.

"She's going to be okay," said Morsixx. "They pumped her stomach of the bottle of aspirin she swallowed. They're going to keep her in an extra day, but they said we could visit, once you woke up."

"You saved us," said Sully.

"I think we all kind of saved each other, Dude. You mom's invited us to dinner next week."

"Sullivan!"

Mom pushed past a nurse to reach his bedside. Her eyes brimmed as she took his hand. For the first time in Sully's memory, she was speechless.

A jab of pain snaked across Sully's skull, and he reached his hand up to cradle the area that hurt.

"It'll grow back, Sullivan," said his mom.

"What will grow?" Sully's fingers crept past matted curls to trace a raised area that ran several inches along the side of his head.

"Your hair. They had to shave that part for the stitches is all," she said. "You saved that girl's life, Sullivan."

"It wasn't just me, Mom."

"I know, dear. Morsixx and I have had lots of time to talk. I was wrong about your friends, Sullivan. He's a lovely young man."

That's two people now who've described Morsixx as lovely. We've clearly crossed into some alternate universe, thought Sully.

Blossom looked tiny and frail when Morsixx wheeled Sully into her room, but her hair haloed her bruised face like the petals of some brilliant flower. In contrast to his own, her hospital gown was bright fuchsia.

"I'm going to stay with my aunt for a while," she said. Morsixx held her hand the way Sully's mom had held his. Well, maybe a bit different than that.

"It's going to be okay." She reached for Sully's hand and squeezed it. "My dad's promised to get help. Both of us are having a hard time with my mom's death. We're going to help each other."

CHAPTER 58

On the way to school on Monday, Sully made a detour onto True Street, surprised to see the fence void of figurines. Puzzled, he scanned the length, and finally located Goyle and The Riddler clinging to the lower rail in an obscure corner. Darth Vader lay in a scrubby patch of weeds at the base of one of the posts.

Sully started along the path to the front door, when Mr. C. gave him a thumbs up from the front window and then pointed toward Perdu Avenue. Following the old man's magnified gaze, Sully saw the missing characters on the top rail at the point where Perdu ended and True began.

Sleeping Beauty and Lancelot sat close together with Pumbaa nearby. Beside them, Charlie Brown stood facing Madonna, who now had a small clump of rainbow-colored putty plugging the hole in her chest. The black pack previously glued to her back was gone.

Sully glanced back at the house as sunlight glinted off Mr. C.'s glasses. Turning back, he found himself face-to-face with the Purse Lady. As if this meeting were prearranged, she put out her hand. Her lips trembled on her left cheek, and her sad eyes surveyed him from opposite sides of her chin.

Sully pulled the rainbow ball out of his pocket and placed it on her palm. As she closed her hand around it, years seemed to fall away from her face, and her features rolled gently into place—still slightly off-kilter, but almost normal.

Miss Winters greeted Sully at the front entrance to the school, almost as if she'd been waiting for him.

"So good to see you this morning, Sullivan." She reached for his hand and clasped it in both of hers. This was clearly a foreign agent in the old lady's skin.

"I am not often wrong, but I have to say I misjudged you, young man. I hope we can start again." Her thin lips widened into a smile that was slightly terrifying.

"Um, okay," said Sully.

"Excellent," she said. "I think you have a very promising future, Sullivan Brewster."

Sully nodded and awkwardly removed his hand from

her grasp. "Thank you, Miss Winters. You, too."

Someone had clearly kidnapped the principal, but he decided to let it ride.

"You've been tricking me!" Winston approached Sully and Morsixx at the locker. "You're that guy! My mom told me."

"I've been trying to tell—"

"Sully," Winston said, as if tasting the name. "I like it. I like you, Sully."

"I like you, too, Winston," Sully said.

"But I don't like him," Winston said.

Sully looked over to where Winston pointed. Tank was cleaning out his locker under the supervision of both Miss Winters and a huge, muscled man Sully surmised was Tank's father. The older version of Tank grabbed his son's forearm and rammed it into the locker, while barking something at him. Tank scowled in Sully's direction. Before Sully turned away, Tank's eyes darted out of sight around the side of his face, as his nose jumped for cover behind one of his ears.

"That's okay, Winston," Sully said, smiling. "He's just a little messed up."

As more and more students poured into the hallways,

the school began to resemble a Mr. Potato Head convention. Dodger's ears bloomed like fungus from his cheekbones, and Ox's mouth gaped sideways between his eyes. Rebecca and Cindy had matching misplaced lips, and even Blake Muir's perfect Greek God nose flapped from side to side on the tip of his chin.

"I guess we all are." Sully patted Winston's back before heading to Sex Ed. "Except maybe for you."

CHAPTER 59

After dinner on Sunday, Blossom insisted on doing dishes with Sully's mom and Eva.

"Dishes were a ritual with me and my mom," she said. "I could use a little 'girl time.' I'll be along in a bit, okay?"

"You got scissors, Dude?"

"What do you want scissors for?"

"You're hurting my eyes, Dude," said Morsixx. "Just come with me for a minute."

Morsixx led Sully to the bathroom and pointed in the mirror. The bald patch on Sully's head looked like a crop circle. "That look no longer works for you. Besides, my mom told me that in our culture, many will cut their hair when there's a death in the family, as a symbol of the loss. It divides things into the before and after. I'm thinking maybe it's time to say goodbye to the old Sully."

Morsixx held the scissors up to Sully's hair.

Sully winced at his reflection. "Do it fast before I change my mind," he said.

"The right side's shorter than the left, Dude," he said after a minute. "I'm going to have to cut more off."

Sully gazed at his reflection. It looked like he'd had a close encounter with a kitchen blender. The pile of hair at his feet sprawled like roadkill.

"Watch out for my nose!" As the blades dove for Sully's bangs, his nose clung to the middle of his face as if on a suicide mission.

"I'm not that bad, Dude."

"Hate to disagree," said Sully.

By the time both sides were somewhat even, Sully's features trembled, with nowhere to hide. His startling hairlessness broadcast his face with alarming shame-lessness.

His right cheekbone was swollen and green, and his lip was split and encrusted with dried blood. His nose, broken in the encounter with Tank, was off-kilter and a little crooked, but other than that, each body part was where it was supposed to be.

He couldn't remember the last time he'd felt so much like himself.

Acknowledgments

I'm grateful to Richard Dionne for pulling Sully out of a half-decade's old pile, thus giving this messed-up kid a chance to show his face.

I'm equally thankful to have had the opportunity to work with Peter Carver as editor. Peter is legend, and was just suspicious enough about my messed-up hero that he asked the tough, insightful questions that helped me reshape Sully's world and wrestle the story under control.

Thank you also to Penny Hozy for copyediting the manuscript so carefully and for providing helpful insight to make it as clean as possible.

The idea for this book was conceived so long ago that I've lost the exact thread of how it came to be at all. Over the years, the story has morphed and evolved, perhaps more than Sully's face. If Sully had actually launched into the world when I first started to write about him, he'd be as old as my son Trysten is now (24). As the before and after of the wrong and right way to deal with bullies, Trysten was the inspiration for both Sully and Morsixx.

My family (JETS: Jeff, Eryn, Trysten and Sarah) lurks not far beneath the surface of everything I write. Sarah and Eryn, my strong, creative, insightful, compassionate daughters, aren't so very hidden behind the tattoos Blossom paints on herself.

A thanks also to the family I grew up in, who were there when I navigated my own choppy waters of high school. My late father, Sid, would have helped Sully find his way. My mother Shirley and brother Geoff are my close friends, and I couldn't ask for two more supportive sisters than my own, JoAnne and Leighanne. Thank you.

Photo credit: JoAnne and Dennis Murphy

Interview with Stephanie Simpson McLellan

Could you tell us where the idea for this story originated?

It's no secret that schoolyard bullying is a reality. I volunteered in my children's classrooms when they were younger, and was dismayed to see that some kids become bullies even in kindergarten. My son is deaf in one ear, which made him appear a little different to others, which in turn made him feel a little unsure of himself. Bullies smell fear and pounce on insecurities, and it took some time for my son to find his way through this. Let's just say that the way he navigated elementary school inspired the character of Sully, and the change in his attitude and feelings about himself, along with the way he reinvented his "look,"* inspired the character of Morsixx.

Between elementary school and high school, my son

(who is a musician) became passionate about heavy metal music. He decided to cut his long, curly brown hair short, dye it black, and change what he wore to reflect the music he loved. Before he cut his hair, he ran a campaign to have people pledge money if he followed through and shaved his head. As a result, he raised over $2,000 for cancer research and donated his hair to make a wig for someone who'd lost their hair because of chemotherapy.

What made you think about the concept of Sully's face rearranging itself as he muddles through the early days of Grade 9?

With the popularity of social media, little is private. Both the good *and* bad things that happen to you—and everything in between—are very public. It's like one giant bulletin board where everything about you is posted for everyone to see. No hiding! We even post emojis to tell people how we're feeling, which is like giving people permission to look into your heart.

The metaphor of Sully's messed-up face plays with how public everything is these days, by taking it out of the digital space and putting it back into the physical world. Sully's misery feels very public to him—so real and uncomfortable that surely everyone must be able to see his fears and insecurities.

But here's something I want you to think about. You learn in the story that Sully is the only one who can actually see his disfiguration (with the exception of The Purse Lady). So, if all your big and little thoughts are poured into social media all the time, does that make you more visible or less so? In other words, when we tell everything to everybody all the time, are as many people really listening as we think, or is there just so much information—too much information for anyone to really take in—that we actually become invisible again?

What led to your deciding to create the set of figurines on Mr. C.'s fence?
True Street is loosely based on a real street in my town that comes off Newmarket's Fairy Lake Park. While I've changed the geography a bit, and bent the exact look and placement of the house on this short street, the real house actually did have a snake-rail fence about a decade ago, to which plastic figurines were affixed and often rearranged. While I never knew (or even saw) the owner, those figurines on the fence intrigued me, and I wondered what motivated someone to do this.

The character of Mr. C. is based on an old man who happened to be on the same tour I was on in Italy, when we visited Pompeii. Like the fictitious Mr. C., this old man relied on canes, wore glasses with impossibly thick lenses, and moved wickedly fast, despite how frail he looked.

You have chosen a number of interesting characters from other stories as models for these figurines. Why did you decide to also include "The Lady of Shalott" among the references Sully comes across in his Grade 9 year?

When Blossom crept into Sully's story, and I thought about what she was struggling with, Tennyson's poem "The Lady of Shalott" instantly came to mind—visually as well as lyrically, as this work has been the inspiration for many paintings. In the poem, the Lady of Shalott lives alone in a tower. She must weave a colorful web and only watch the outside world through a mirror. If she looks at the real world of Camelot directly, she will die. When her mirror breaks, leaving even her reflection of the world fractured, she leaves the tower and floats down the river in a boat to her death. In her way, Blossom is also unable to look directly at her real world, because it has become too painful. Instead of weaving tapestries to imitate life, Blossom paints an artificial life on herself.

Sometimes we discover that the bully has himself been a victim of abuse—Tank is an example of that. But what do you think leads kids like Dodger and Ox to participate in harassing Sully?

I guess the question is, how do any gangs form? Bullies usually have sidekicks—both in movies / comics and in the real world—as I guess it's easier and safer to side with power than to fight against it. Certainly, we're living at a time when many are confusing authoritarian power with leadership and strength. If you study what makes someone a bully, you'll find that a bully attacks someone they see as weak, and they do this so they don't have to think about their own insecurities and weaknesses. After all, as the saying goes, the best defense is a good offense. The themes of exposure and reflection run through the novel. Bullies and their sidekicks likely don't do the hard work of self-reflection. Ox and Dodger use Tank as their mirror—they see themselves reflected in what they perceive as his strength.

While Sully becomes the target of Tank and his friends, somehow Morsixx does not. Why do you think that is?

As I mentioned, the character of Morsixx was inspired by the person my son became in Grade 9. Thinking about the motives and characters of his previous tormentors, he came to realize that their selection of a victim wasn't really personal, and that by cowering, he was giving the bullies what they needed—a victim. He was offering himself up as victim.

Eleanor Roosevelt said, "No one can make you feel inferior without your consent." In the book, I say that "Morsixx's armor is that he doesn't care." Morsixx himself says his father "broke himself on other people's arrows." I'm not saying bullies can't gain power over others (history gives us enough of those examples), but I believe that on a personal level, you can shrink a bully's power by refusing to consent to the opinion they have of you. Decide that their opinion is not valid and then live that.

While Tank has become a bully because of the treatment he's experienced from his father, Blossom disdains bullying and becomes one of Sully's protectors. How do you explain her being able to rise above what is happening to her at home?

Blossom's strength has roots in the strong and loving family she had before her mother died. While her father lost his way with alcohol in his grief, we know that Blossom's life was not always this way. In other words, she knows the difference and remains strong, believing she can put things back the way she knows they could be. That's part of it. But the other part is that Blossom's very mature, take-charge attitude is one of the common personality roles taken on by a child of an alcoholic. Some children of alcoholics adopt the role of Clown (to reduce household stress through humor), while others become the Scapegoat (blamed for the family problems), or Lost Child (who escapes household anxiety by becoming invisible). Blossom embodies a fourth alternative, which is the role of Hero. In a situation where the addicted parent is not fulfilling their role as responsible adult, the Hero child steps in to try to fill that space; to create control where there is none. As Blossom finds herself increasingly unable to change her own situation, she takes Sully under her wing. If she cannot save herself, perhaps she can save someone else.

While it's not surprising that among those we meet in school there are bullies who are more or less our own age (like Tank, Dodger, and Ox), Sully also has to deal with adults who have little understanding or sympathy for his situation—and they are educators who should be ready to support him. Why did you want to include Mr. Green and Miss Winter as characters in this story?

School is just a microcosm of life and the world at large. There are good and bad people everywhere. I had many brilliant teachers at school who inspired me (a shout-out to my Grade 7 teacher, Mr. Tellier), and I also had others who weren't quite so wonderful. Ms. Wippet is one of the good ones; a teacher who is not only passionate about what she teaches, but someone who sees her students. I wish a Ms. Wippet for all my readers.

But I also think it's important to show the range of good and not-so-good, so that if a student meets the self-absorbed indifference of a Mr. Green or the self-important harshness of a Miss Winters, they don't assume there's nowhere else to turn. Just because you are an adult and a teacher doesn't mean you have everything all figured out (both Mr. Green and Miss Winters end up learning from their students). At the same time, I believe every student reading this will have one or several really gifted human beings as teachers in their school, if they open their eyes to look for them.

This is your first published novel, and it deals with a difficult theme. What advice do you have for young people who want to write their own stories about ideas or experiences that haven't been easy to deal with?

For me, writing has always been a way of processing my thoughts, good and bad. I have a trunk full of diaries from when I was a kid. Often, the processing we need to do is over the hard stuff, as we try to make sense of things and find a way to deal with hard situations. In between the living and the writing is the stuff that builds our characters, and sometimes stories emerge.

I would encourage young people to take their hard stuff—write it down, flip it upside down, and turn it inside out. What falls out is called learning. Can you re-write the way you feel about something bad that happened to you, because you've taken the time to think and process? Can what you learned help someone else do a little of their own self-reflection? Can what you write become someone else's springboard? Stories come from life. Your life has stories that may be worth telling.

Many kids find the move from elementary to high school difficult. For some, like Sully, the challenge may seem too difficult to explain to parents or others in their families. Do you know of resources available to young people who need support and encouragement at such times?

Whether you're in high school, elementary or middle school, if you need someone to help you through feelings of anxiety and isolation, please reach out to one of these resources who will help you:

- Kids Help Phone (Canada): 1-800-668-6868
- National Suicide Prevention Hotline (U.S.): 1-800-273-8255 (1-800-273-TALK)
- Crisis Text Line:
  - US & UK: Text Hello to 741741
  - Canada: Text Hello to 686868

Thank you, Stephanie, for your insights and information.